Anything
to Look Hot

Anything
^{to} Look Hot

Candid Confessions of a Plastic Surgeon

Jas Kohli

Srishti
PUBLISHERS & DISTRIBUTORS

Srishti Publishers & Distributors
Registered Office: N-16, C.R. Park
New Delhi – 110 019
Corporate Office: 212A, Peacock Lane
Shahpur Jat, New Delhi – 110 049
editorial@srishtipublishers.com

First published by
Srishti Publishers & Distributors in 2015

For Dr. Harbhajan Kohli
&
Mr. Manmohan Singh
....we miss your fatherly presence.

Acknowledgements

Plastic surgery is a unique branch because most of the patients are not weighed down by any 'disease'. Therefore one can have the liberty of talking to them jovially. I am indebted to all my patients who took minor complications in their stride, tolerated my excessive sermonizing and waited patiently for me when I took too long for a procedure.

Through these years, I have interacted with so many junior and senior colleagues. Thanks for demonstrating all of your good and bad qualities and techniques, so that I could choose which ones to follow.

I am thankful to Dr. S P Bajaj, Dr. P S Chari, Dr. R K Sharma, Dr R P Narayan, Dr. V K Tiwari, Dr. Gautam Biswas, and other teachers, who have emphasized on professional excellence as well as compassionate patient care.

Although writing a fiction book is more or less a solitary expedition, a lot of support and encouragement is needed to forge ahead, especially through the rough patches. The immediate family members always bear the brunt of the writer's love affair with words. Despite one's best efforts to the contrary, one always tends to cut up on family time. So, I do appreciate them for standing by me.

My mom, Dr. Sunder Kohli, is an epitome of courage in personal life and dedication to the medical profession. She is touching eighty but still working full time. My wife, Dr. Bela has not only been very supportive, but has also tolerated my aberrant sleep cycle for so long. Her total involvement in patient care is an inspiration to me. Thanks are due to my son Nishant for constantly pushing and prodding me to make progress, and my daughter Kavya for spreading cheer at home.

I am indebted to my friends Vikas Singhle and Rajeel Singhle, for keeping up my morale during the period of struggle. I still remember Vikas's words – People can even find god by trying hard. So, persist and you will succeed as a writer.

I thank Mita Kapur and Kanishka Gupta for their help in polishing the text. Their comments felt quite acerbic initially, but seem so sweet now.

The publisher at Srishti, Arup Bose, has taken keen personal interest in every aspect of the book, which means that my worries can shift to other avenues of my life.

My editor Stuti, who has been instrumental in giving the book its final shape, is as meticulous as a plastic surgeon. I also thank the rest of the team at Srishti Publishers. Also, Wasim Helal has come out with an excellent cover design.

Above all, I thank god for bestowing me with a surgeon's hands and a writer's mind.

You can send feedback and share your views with me at drjskohli@gmail.com, or follow me on Facebook for more on the book.

Reaching for the Stars

The eye of a falcon, the courage of a tiger, the composure of a monk, the versatility of a decathlete, the concentration of a marksman, the endurance of a mountaineer and hands as deft as a lady's – these are the attributes of a good surgeon.

These lines have constantly pushed me to rise above mediocrity. Yet, that evening, I was a bundle of nerves. The results of the entrance test for the M.Ch. (Master of Chirurgiae) course were to be declared the next morning and I wanted to kill two birds with one stone. There was my desire to be a plastic surgeon, the only person licensed to sculpt other human beings, and the subconscious desire to get even with Manika who had ditched me and who deserved to regret not having a personal plastic surgeon for life!

The next morning, I set off on my scooter, whipped by gusts of the *loo*, Delhi's hot wind. By the time I entered the South Campus my heart beat seemed to have amplified into the beat of a large drum. The notice boards were inaccessible as the doctors were jostling to have a look at their future. I thought of elbowing my way in but it was not necessary. In a few moments, a small mob had gathered around me.

'Hey, you *topped* and that too by a wide margin,' Girish, my old classmate, shouted.

My daze gave way to euphoria. I lost count of the handshakes and hugs. But the greeting I relished the most was that of Mantav, the self-styled top seed. His smile was fake, the lines of laughter only visible on the lower half of his face. It was understandable: his overblown ego had suddenly been burst.

I needed to share my joy with my parents so I rushed back to my flat. Dad was sitting in the veranda, his face hidden behind a newspaper. He had probably expected me to come back with a long face.

'I did it!' I shouted, touching his feet.

Dad hugged me, his thick moustache seeming to sway with joy. It was a momentous occasion in the life of a person who had suffered heavily due to the partition of the country. At this juncture, I was his only hope of helping the family rise from the lower middle class.

Mom, whom I had nicknamed 'Mother India' for always putting family above the self, kissed me on the forehead. I had fought with her only once and that too because she had handed over some of my important notes to the junk dealer for the princely sum of a hundred and forty rupees.

The first call was naturally to my sister, Bhavya. At that time, night had already coaxed most of Chicago into a deep slumber. She answered the phone in a drowsy voice, but on hearing of my achievement, jumped right out of bed.

'I am thrilled,' she said. 'Finally, you've made the family proud. I can't call you the "hollow headed man" anymore!'

'Deal,' I replied. 'And I'll stop labelling you "tear factory", even though you'll always remain that!'

'This is not the time for silly fights. Will the two of you ever grow up?' Mom said. But she seemed pleased that both her children had retained their childhood bond, even if it was based on teasing and banter.

Then, there was a call from my cousin, Pinky.

'Bhaiya, please do an advance booking to correct my parrot beak nose,' she said excitedly.

'Wait till you are eighteen,' I said, 'by which time, your face, nose as well as your brain will have fully developed.'

As more greetings poured in, I revelled in my achievement. But, even in my moment of glory, I could not help reflecting on the tyranny of the exam system. In the name of competition, it had caused seventy screwed up faces for just two overjoyed ones.

By evening, our house was full of boisterous relatives and friends. An impromptu celebration has its own charm. There were no hassles in making arrangements as a couple of eating joints in the nearby market did home delivery. My doctor friends had nicknamed the H Block Market the 'Heart Attack Block' as the *dhabas* here, which dished out fat-rich food, seemed to have been financed by the cardiology departments of various hospitals. My patients, who I often lectured on avoiding excessive fat intake, would have been horrified if they saw me consistently wolf down the keema naan with extra butter at Lazeez Dhaba!

There were a few Yuppies but they were easily outnumbered by the Puppies (prosperous urban Punjabis), a community which believes that subtlety is the biggest crime! The tandoori chicken awaited its last ritual bath in whisky. After some casual conversation, boasting about property and promiscuity took over.

Dad's cousin, Suresh, downed a few large pegs quickly to achieve a respectable level of drunkenness. Once his eyes were sufficiently red, his tongue began to wag. He talked to me in a loud voice, so that everyone paid attention.

'*Oye* Dhruv. Take charge of our ageing faces. But do a reverse facelift on Narinder. Create more wrinkles on his face!'

To confuse me further, he maintained a poker face. Narinder, Suresh's target, was Dad's younger brother.

It was one of the weirdest demands of my whole surgical career. I had never read or heard about anything called reverse facelift surgery.

'But why so?' I asked.

'As Narinder is growing older, he is getting more and more girlfriends!' Suresh grinned.

Then, he broke into peals of uproarious laughter. Narinder's wife, Sunita, initially looked to be in a tizzy. But, she too started laughing after realizing that the whisky was directing Suresh's performance.

The party ended well past midnight. I went to the terrace to watch my favourite show: the night sky. To me it seemed like a lovely woman in a classy black gown. That night, the usual city haze was fortunately not there. I focused my gaze to the top of the sky dome and was rewarded with the sight of some constellations – Lyra, Hercules and Cygnus.

Perhaps I was destined to be an astronomer. After my birth, my paternal aunt Nirmala had been given the honour of naming me. She had called me Dhruv, 'the Pole Star'. How could I know there would be such a burden to live up to my name?

When I was around five, each day unveiled new discoveries. I used to fire all the queries at my mom, in the belief that she was an encyclopaedia. One evening, I asked her the meaning of my name. After nightfall, she took me to the terrace and showed me the Pole Star. I was catapulted into a magical kingdom high above the earth.

'Why did *Bua* name me after this star?' I asked.

'Dhruv is the only fixed star whereas all the others keep rotating. Since time immemorial it has guided sailors and travellers. Bua wanted you to become as famous as the Pole Star,' Mom replied.

'What does "famous" mean?'

'A lot of people recognize and respect a famous person.'

'What is respect?'

'You will understand when you grow up. Let's go to sleep now, no more questions,' Mom said, putting an end to her viva voce!

That was the beginning of my incurable passion for astronomy.

Two weeks later, it was time to join the department. After looking at the Arogyam Hospital building, I was filled with enthusiasm. After all, it was going to be my home for at least the next two years.

On the way to the plastic surgery department, a spicy scent hit me. It was not a Christian Dior eau de toilette, but disinfectant fumes, unpleasant to most, but uplifting to me.

At around eleven, the head of department called me to his chamber. In the corridor outside his office, I noticed the framed black and white photos of the old heads, some of who had already completed their earthly journey, but whose spirits seemed to linger in the department they had nurtured with great dedication.

Dr. Vidur, the head, was engrossed in a journal, seated behind a huge table covered with books and files. It was obvious he got a high on a cocktail of academics and authority. With his grey hair, the deep lines on his forehead, and a long, thin upper lip, he looked a typical academic don. I noticed that a large garlanded image of Sai Baba dwarfed all his framed certificates.

Raising his bushy eyebrows, he asked me to sit.

'Thank you, sir.'

'You need to answer a question before you can begin,' he said, harshly.

Was this a further evaluation after the entrance test, I wondered.

'Right, sir,' I replied and braced myself.

'What is the definition of a militant?' he asked, casually.

I was flabbergasted. A weird question had been put to me instead of a query related to medical science.

I replied, 'Militants use violence to achieve their political ends.'

The chief's expression remained glum, implying that I had not hit the nail on the head.

'A militant sacrifices his personal comforts and family life in pursuit of his goal. To become a good plastic surgeon, you must have the zeal of a militant. Now get to work right away,' he said, smiling. His words gave me the energy to get through the next two years.

I rushed out of the office. While walking the corridors of the department, my mind drifted to the memory of my previous residency. I had pursued an MS in the department of surgery in the Prime Medical Institute during the last three years. There, I had to work under Dr. Neel Kamal, a perfectionist. On the last day, I had felt as elated as a slave who was being set free. However, fate had intervened and I was taking the plunge into choppy waters by choice, yet again.

Dr. Neel Kamal used to say, 'Trial by fire is justified in residency. The training in medical sciences is the toughest because you get a license to treat a human being. Even a minor error could make the patient's life a living hell. The residents feel that they are exploited by making them work for up to eighteen hours a day. Often, their sleep is also cut. However, the ability to bear physical hardships is required in many situations later on.'

But, I felt that there was another aspect to this. The seniors wanted the juniors to have a taste of the troubles they had undergone in their own residency days. So, the vicious circle continued. But it was difficult to call a spade a spade in front of the chief.

A beautiful lady doctor crossed my path. She reminded me of Manika, my colleague during the first two years of MS. I used to admire the pretty girl for her boldness in venturing into a male dominated field. Her colourful dresses broke the monotony of brown, black and grey. We already knew each other since she had been my junior in medical college. Sparks flew and we ended up making love.

However, three weeks later, she told me there had been a marriage proposal from an NRI doctor and she had agreed to it. I was shocked. It was obvious that Manika had been lured by the American dream. She even left her residency midway. Anyway, she would have had to do it all over again in the US. I felt I had been used as a pit stop in her drive towards her destination.

I imagined her husband saying to me, 'I have a dream house in a suburb, a Chevrolet Corvette and the American citizenship to lure your girl. What do you have?'

I had a fitting reply: '*Mere paas maa hai, meri Bharat mata*! I have my motherland!'

However, she and I separated amicably. In our last meeting, we cherished our time together. I promised not to contact her, for the sake of her marriage. The very next day I had an intense urge to call her, but there was nothing I could do about it.

Hiding my face behind a beard, I took on a fake Devdas-like avatar. Instead of hitting the bottle, I lost myself in *Hum ko kiske gham ne mara* and other ghazals about crushed love. Wallowing in self pity gave me a strange pleasure.

After struggling for a few months, I was finally able to put her out of my mind. I resolved to take revenge by becoming 'something'.

I also remembered the incident that had occurred just after I had passed my MS.

'Beta, you have got your degree. It is high time you get married,' my mother said to me, concerned.

'If you agree, I will start putting out matrimonial ads,' she added.

'Listen to the ad I drafted,' my father said. 'Required medico girl from an illustrious family. She should be amicable, tall and exceptionally beautiful. No bars.'

I chuckled. 'Dad, you've omitted an important point, her IQ should be above 150!'

'Stop it, Dhruv! Have some consideration for us. I feel ashamed almost every day when everyone asks me why I am not marrying you off,' Mom said.

'Tell them to stop interfering with our personal affairs. Mom, the entrance exam for M.Ch. in plastic surgery is just three months away. Can't all this wait till then?'

My parents had no answer to this one. They knew I had to apply myself wholeheartedly to crack the tough entrance test.

A few days later, as I reached home, I was in for a surprise. My parents had called their distant relatives, the Gakhars. My mother thought their daughter Sonika would be the ideal daughter-in-law.

'Just talk to Sonika for a while. We are not forcing you to make any commitment,' Mom said.

I entered the living room and greeted everyone. Sonika was very beautiful. As her alluring eyes met mine, my resistance crumbled. Both of us were told to move to another room, obviously so we could assess each other first hand.

'I did my B.Com from Lady Shri Ram College and attended the Etiquette Finishing School,' Sonika said. I felt quite lucky to have stumbled upon a girl who gave me such positive vibes and could carry off a *sari* as well as a midi.

'So what's your favourite pastime, apart from cutting up hapless people?' she asked.

'I am into Astronomy,' I told her. 'Since the last six years, I have my own telescope.'

Her eyes opened wide with excitement. I presumed that her complete surrender to me was just a formality.

She showed me her palms and said, 'Great! Tell me something about my future?'

'I can tell that we're not made for each other,' I said.

She was dumbfounded. I politely asked her to move to the living room, where our parents were waiting with bated breath. My morose face was a giveaway. The Gakhars made a dignified exit, pretending they hadn't been interested either.

'What went wrong? The girl is pretty and well educated,' Mom said angrily.

'She has a lot of certificates, yes, but she is not mentally compatible with me. How can I marry someone who can't tell astronomy from astrology,' I said.

Even after that episode, my parents did not give up. They kept making the rounds of deities, holy men and soothsayers. However, they ended up poorer by thousands of bucks with no daughter-in-law in sight!

The Wretched Resident Again

My chain of thought was broken as I bumped into my senior, Dr. Bhuvan.

'Come, I will show you around the department,' he said.

The senior resident had already pocketed the M.Ch. degree and it showed in his unhurried walk and unruffled talk. The seniors were supposed to be the nicest to the new residents during the first few days. I felt like a yak which was being pampered and fattened to carry heavy loads over high Himalayan passes.

'The first funda of residency is that you will get overt praise once in a blue moon. If your day goes by without being yelled at, it means you have been appreciated for doing your job well,' Dr. Bhuvan said.

Then he instructed me on my tasks, stressing more on the don'ts. I was also introduced to Venkat, who had been selected in the entrance test along with me.

Dr. Bhuvan continued, 'The department has three units, each headed by a senior consultant. Next are the junior consultants, also from the creamy layer. The resident doctors are responsible for most of the work. At the bottom are the junior residents, the fresh MBBS graduates who remain for six months to a year. They do not get any degree but are given experience certificates.

The junior residents have to be closely supervised by the seniors since they are greenhorns.'

'What about the chief?'

'Well, he is the most important person in the department because he has the overall responsibility – not just for treating and teaching, but taming, too! Even after stints in hospitals in France, UK and the United States, his *desi* English accent has stubbornly clung to him. But Dr. Vidur is famous in the academic circles as he has invented quite a few plastic surgery procedures.'

On my first day in the department, I attended the grand round that was compulsory for all consultants and junior doctors. From the start, the chief directed most of his questions at me. I put in my best but was soon clean bowled after fumbling over a basic query.

'You are not even fit to be a surgeon, leave alone a plastic surgeon. It seems that you sent an impersonator to the entrance test,' the chief said.

I noticed all the doctors smiling, including Venkat. They were obviously enjoying the entertainment. It hurt like hell; just a few days ago, I had been hailed as a role model.

But there was a lot to be absorbed from the chief regarding patient care. Dr. Vidur greeted patients by their name and listened to them carefully. He checked the charts in detail and also confirmed the compliance with previous orders. The nursing staff and junior doctors were kept on their toes.

The next day, Venkat presented a seminar on the role of stem cells in plastic surgery. He had thoroughly prepared for it by spending the previous evening in the National Medical Library.

'Well done,' the chief said, immediately after the presentation.

A compliment from him was very rare.

Afterwards, we started with the morning rounds. Venkat seemed to be on an ego trip. However, he missed a clear cut fracture on a facial X-ray at the first bed itself. We expectantly looked at the chief for a sarcastic comment. He did not disappoint us.

'I think Venkat himself needs an injection of basic concepts, and that too for many sessions!' he said.

It was sweet revenge with no effort on my part. I smiled while Venkat's sunny face became downcast.

The chief took an introductory lecture about the basics of plastic surgery.

He started, 'There are a lot of misconceptions among the public about the meaning of the term, "plastic surgery". Plastic-like material is used as an implant, in only a small percentage of cases. The term is actually derived from the Greek word "plastikos", which means to mould. Our department has a saying: Make the sullen mirrors of your patients turn friendly!'

We were then taught how to study facial features.

'Try to analyze different faces to develop an aesthetic sense,' the chief told us.

From that day, Venkat and I turned into compulsive observers, especially of pretty faces, but only with an academic intent!

As soon as I entered my hostel room in the evening, I stood in front of the mirror. Because of the newly imbibed knowledge, I was able to evaluate my face objectively. Most features were in proportion. I could pass as a model...well, almost. What spoilt it were the bags under the eyes. I had also turned out to be few inches shorter than my six-footer dad. But it was difficult to buy Dad's explanation that his impressive physique was because of milk, drunk straight from the cow, during his childhood!

The next day, we were in the operation theatre. The list of operations included reshaping of the face, nose, breasts, etc. There were also cases for reconstructive surgery, for treating burns, injuries and birth defects.

When I entered the OT, I felt at home. Familiar scenes started playing. The staff and the doctors entered the changing room and put on their theatre dresses, caps and masks. I had to wear a dress belonging to a woman, as mine was not ready yet. But, looking like a transvestite for one day was a small price to pay for becoming a plastic surgeon.

That day, like most other operation days, there were a few challenging cases on the list. The easier surgeries were called '*malai*' cases. Every trainee surgeon wanted to grab them. But, the hardworking ones were often piped to the post by the sycophants!

The first surgery was on a child, with a birth defect of the ear. The upper part of his ear was folded in on itself.

In one of the side rooms, two huge autoclaves were hissing like a dragon and spewing steam. The operation theatre technicians and staff had begun their work well before the arrival of the surgical team. Mamta, the in-charge, was arranging the gleaming steel instruments on a trolley.

As the chief entered, he asked her, 'Is everything ready?'

'Yes sir.'

The chief quickly scanned the instrument trolley.

'Your trolley is incomplete without the key instrument, the Cat's Paw Retractor. This is not expected from senior staff,' the chief frowned.

'Sorry sir. I will get it.'

The chief pointed towards me and then said to Mamta, 'You are giving some serious competition to these residents where inefficiency is concerned.'

I was not safe, even as a bystander!

The child was brought inside and the initiation of anaesthesia was smooth. Then, Dr. Vidur took over. He chanted, *'Om Sai Ram,'* and asked Mamta to hand him the knife. After making the initial incisions, he looked at the residents assisting him and said, 'Nobody does it better!'

'Just a few minutes after invoking the name of God, he is proclaiming himself to be a sort of deity,' I thought.

But that was not surprising as I had come across only a few modest surgeons in my career. Most of them tried to convey that they had been bestowed with the most dexterous hands by God. It did not stop at that. Other surgeons were thought to be crappy and their surgery was often referred to as butchery! Some went to the extent of referring to their archrivals as 'man-eaters'.

The moment my grip on the retractor loosened from fatigue, I received a slap on the wrist from the chief.

'Concentrate! The way we operate for two hours will determine how the boy will feel about himself for the rest of his life. We have to give a hundred percent,' he said.

I did not mind his strong arm tactics because teachings which were combined with rebukes were likely to be retained the longest. Dr. Vidur sculpted the cartilage to make the ear look nearly normal. When the surgery was about to end I was told to put skin stitches on the back of the ear. My hands began trembling because of the chief's stern gaze.

'Dhruv! You are handling the tissue roughly. Be as gentle with it as you would be with your girlfriend!' Dr Vidur said.

The chief took the instrument from me and demonstrated the proper technique.

After the surgery, it was time to bring the child out of anaesthesia. As the child declared consciousness by crying, everyone smiled.

'There are two occasions when the cry of a child delights. One is at the time of birth, and the other is at the end of a surgery. In anaesthesia, the starting and end are crucial just like the takeoff and landing of an aeroplane,' Dr. Raman, the anaesthesiologist, said to the resident doctors.

'You may be piloting many flights, but our job is even tougher. Every day, we drive in many formula one races!' Dr. Vidur added.

The next day was my first twenty-four hour duty. The night shift was invariably hectic; there was a constant inflow of emergencies. I was groggy even after two cups of coffee. After midnight, sleep was seductive.

But, within a few days, I got used to my job and was also assimilated into the doctor fraternity. The all-embracing capital had attracted doctors from all corners of the country. Here, national integration was not just limited to social synergy. Doctors from different states were marrying each other and stirring up the national gene pool.

Duty in the burn ward was the toughest. Spending a few hours there was like getting a glimpse of hell on earth. The dressing of a single patient took up to two hours and by the time it finished, the dresser himself felt sick. Moreover, we as doctors knew that some of the extensive burn patients were destined to die.

Most of the bills for poor patients were paid by the hospital. However, the relatives often had to take loans, mostly from informal sources even for the modest expenses required for medicines. One incident was particularly upsetting. A man from Jispur village abandoned his burnt wife. He told the staff nurse on duty that the amount required for treatment could fetch him a new bride.

I was also introduced to an exciting new technology in our department. While I was on emergency duty, Dr. Vidur surprised everyone by showing up unannounced at eleven in the night.

He told us to summon all the doctors immediately. Casualties were expected at any moment.

A few minutes later, screams were heard from the casualty. Everyone rushed towards the area. Seven patients were brought in. They were all gasping for breath, although there were no injuries or burns on their bodies. Two of them were frenetically trying to contact their relatives on mobile handsets, which I had noticed for the first time.

'Quick! Start oxygen in all cases,' the chief shouted at the top of his voice.

This caused frenzy amongst the staff. They hastily opened the regulators on the oxygen pipelines and cylinders.

Even the laziest of doctors reached the department in no time. Within a few minutes of starting oxygen, there was a drastic improvement in the condition of all the patients.

After the situation was under control, the chief explained, 'There was a fire in the nearby cinema. A lot of people were trapped. Their respiratory systems were affected due to the poisonous gases released from the burning upholstery.'

Meanwhile, another five casualties arrived. However, to our horror, all of them were lifeless masses of flesh. If only they had made it to us a few minutes earlier, they would have survived. One of them had a mobile phone clasped between the thumb and index finger.

Much to my chagrin, instead of grieving the dead, I was visualizing the mobile phone models. I wondered if I was becoming thick skinned after having seen lots of injuries and deaths during my surgical career.

The next day, the disaster made the headlines in all newspapers. Since it had been an expensive premier, all the cinema goers were the very well off, who could afford mobiles and their exorbitant call rates.

Most of my colleagues were workaholics. But there were a few shirkers too. They were constantly devising sly strategies to offload their share of jobs onto others. So, the sincere types were rewarded with more work! It was disquieting to know that some doctors looked upon the patients as objects that they were being trained on.

One day, I was seething with anger at one such character, Shishir. He had left night duty without completing many of his tasks.

I went to Dr. Mohan, the consultant of the unit.

'Sir, I have murderous feelings for Shishir, the worst doctor I have ever come across. He shuns patient care but tries to grab as many surgeries as possible.'

'Never be disgusted by a person. Hate only his or her bad qualities. In fact, nobody is totally good or completely awful. I will ensure that Shishir mends his ways.'

Dr. Mohan's words equipped me to deal with many thorny situations later in life. I stopped classifying everyone as good or bad and could also deal with other people's irrational behaviour in a better way. If I am wronged, I still curse the perpetrator in my mind, but with milder abuses!

With his messy hair, Dr. Mohan looked like a mad scientist. Despite doing few cosmetic surgeries, his renown was far and wide. He was into microsurgery, the branch of plastic surgery that has advanced beyond what science fiction speculates. With the help of his operating microscope, Dr. Mohan miraculously rejoined limbs, hands and fingers. He could even solve the loss of a penis due to injury or cancer.

'I am married to microsurgery,' Dr. Mohan often said.

My senior Nayan told me that once Dr. Mohan had to stay in the hospital for forty-eight hours at a stretch due to a series of emergencies. When he reached home on the third day, his son Naman said to him, 'Uncle, who do you want to see in this house?'

Whenever I assisted in marathon microsurgeries, I ended up taking a pain killer.

The chief's favourite take on Dr. Mohan was summed up in these words, 'This microsurgeon is so calm that he would be unperturbed even if there was a fire under his chair!'

Dr. Vidur often narrated a story. Once, while moving around in the hospital, Dr. Mohan was lost in thought and hit a wall. Thinking that he had bumped into a doctor, he said, 'Sorry.' On looking up, he noticed the wall but again instinctively said sorry to the wall!

Dr. Salil, the star of the department, was the third unit's consultant. The James Bond look-alike could pass as a plastic surgeon from Beverly Hills. Predictably, most youngsters flocked to him. He had been renowned as the Casanova of his batch in medical college. He would take up the enviable responsibility of dropping all the girls of his class to railway station during the vacations. His better half was none other than supermodel and former Miss Delhi, Chaahat, who often created furore in the department by appearing in mini-skirts.

With time, interesting anecdotes of the junior and senior doctors were revealed to me. Just like folk tales, these had been passed on through word of mouth by generations of doctors and spiced up over the previous versions. If only they had been properly documented, an epic would have been created.

I hit it off well with Venkat, my batchmate. We exchanged duties whenever required and also shared our study material. Initially, we were posted in different wards. He used to finish his work much quicker than me. One day, I confronted him.

'Today, I will not leave you till you tell me your secret.'

'Simple. Learn to delegate. Make use of people. Just like an multi-level marketing company, get more hands and minds to work for you. I have noticed that by rushing everywhere, you put yourself in time pressure. However, if I am occupied, I catch hold of hospital staff moving to other floors and request them to do the needful. I also have a way with the ladies! So the staff nurses go out of their way to help me out with ward jobs.'

'Got it. Smart work always scores over hard work,' I said.

The ward was like our living room, while the duty room doubled as a party zone. When the going got tough, the best escape was a quick visit to the cafeteria. Harried residents, who had just received an unfair scolding from a consultant, often hit back at him with swear words, many of them unmentionable.

Like in my previous residency, I was forced to become an anti-social element! I told my cousins and friends that I was unavailable for unproductive activities like loitering and gossiping. Most Bollywood blockbusters, including some landmark movies, passed me by. But Dad was still queuing up on Fridays for the first shows and sometimes even bought tickets from black marketers.

Due to the reforms in the economy, my relatives and friends had got big increases in their salaries. They were switching their core branches and flourishing even more after they had. But I had to stay put.

One weekend, I got a call from my cousin Sameer.

'Break away from your sick routine. Let's go to Disco 22 this Saturday.'

'Sorry, I have an emergency duty that day.'

I lied as I didn't have a girl to cavort with me. I couldn't even afford the entry fee, booze or food.

The next day, I told Dr. Vidur, 'Sir, this is so unfair. Most of my cousins and friends, who are less qualified than me, have already settled so well.'

'To enjoy your profession, you have to see it in a different light. It will give you a lot of satisfaction, respect and prestige. Even money will follow, but a bit later.' I appreciated his words a few days later. I bumped into my schoolmate Ranjit after a gap of thirteen years. He had come to visit a relative who was in for a plastic surgery. We went to the cafeteria to catch up. In a short period, he had taken his family business to a new level by adding a steel rolling mill.

I said, 'Here I am. Still studying and training on a basic stipend. I keep on reducing my parents' burden by making their wallets lighter! Do you know I have covered the two dents in my car with stickers?'

I was trying to elicit a few words of sympathy and consolation.

'I would love to swap places with you. My factories might be having a turnover in tens of crores but I crave a meaningful life. You are lucky to be in a position where every action is geared towards someone's good. One day you will realize that the true power is with you.'

From that day, a new serenity took over as I stopped envying other people's astronomical salaries. But, guys have many other things to compare. My face used to turn crimson when cute girls enveloped my friends in their arms while sitting pillion on their motorcycles. To rub salt into my wounds, these chaps deliberately braked hard frequently so that pretty pillion riders' breasts massaged their back.

Hard work aided by touches of sycophancy turned me into the chief's blue-eyed boy. Sometimes, he would even indulge in friendly chatter. However, the next day, a single mistake could turn him into a raging bull. The angry young man of yore, instead of mellowing, had seamlessly moved to turn into an angry old man.

He had a ready explanation for his bouts of fury.

'To be an effective head of department, I have to combine *Gandhigiri* with *dadagiri*!'

The chief also began trusting me to attend to his cosmetic surgery patients, most of whom were well-heeled.

One such case was Sonya, a model, who was admitted for liposuction of her flanks and hips. The surgery went well but post-operatively, she bugged the chief a lot. Every time he went on his rounds, she welcomed him with a brand new set of complaints.

Dr. Vidur called for me.

'Dhruv, Sonya is all yours. She seems to be allergic to old people like me.'

I went to her room and greeted her with a wide smile.

'Dr. Vidur is occupied in official work today. So I will look after you. How are you doing today?'

'Better than yesterday.'

'I have seen your pictures in magazines, and it feels great to meet you in person. In fact, even the hospital linen dress looks like haute couture on you!'

'Doc, this is the height of complimenting! Anyway, thanks. You made me smile.'

'See you tomorrow.'

'Before you go, please write down a prescription on my chart,' she said.

'All the required medicines are already being given.'

'Please write "Dr. Dhruv twice a day". You are the most effective medicine for me!' she said.

'The proper dose would be thrice a day then! Bye.'

As I came out of her room, I could not believe my luck. She seemed to have been bowled over by my charm. Actually, a model could not ask for a better companion than a plastic surgeon, the preserver of looks. That way, I did have a fair chance of emulating Dr. Salil by having a beauty queen as my girlfriend.

The next morning, I came half an hour early, to give her an increased dose of my company. As soon as I entered her room, I found that a square-faced hunk was in my way. I prayed that he would turn out to be her brother since good looks ran in families.

'Good morning Dr. Dhruv. This is my boyfriend, Jayesh. He has come specially from Bangalore,' she said.

I do not even remember the conversation after that as I struggled to maintain my sanity. But I did keep my promise of visiting her thrice daily, till she was discharged. Despite being taken for a nasty ride, I still feel that plastic surgeons and models would make great couples.

I faced another ticklish situation in the private ward a few days later. A girl in late teens was admitted for the correction of a broad nasal tip. The spirited Vaishali did not show any sign of pre-surgery blues. However, all hell broke loose when she spotted her neighbours in the department. They had brought their son for treatment of facial injuries. She immediately covered her face with a handkerchief.

She said, 'Doctor, those people live near my house. If they spot me, tell them that I have suffered an injury to my nose.'

'Come on! You have not committed a crime. Anyway, I will shift you to another floor.'

Once she was moved, the chief said, 'Our covertness should surpass even that of the government agencies hiding the nukes! I have operated on people living in the same street but made sure that they never got to know of each other's surgery. This way, we do not get enough word of mouth publicity. However, there are few loudmouths who announce that they have been shaped by the scalpel of a plastic surgeon. They are our moving pamphlets.'

Later, the chief called us into his office. We were all ears as he explained his philosophy of dealing with the patients.

'The plastic surgery patient has to be handled with care because the results are subjective. A number of pre-surgery counseling sessions might have to be undertaken. This will bring out their wants as well as fears.'

'But sir, if we tell them the potential complications in detail, wouldn't that scare most patients?' Venkat asked.

'One should discuss the expected result as well as complications, frankly, even at the cost of losing a few cases. Often, the plastic surgeon is jubilant after doing an excellent technical job. But, the patient feels miserable as the results are not up to his or her expectation. That is due to a communication gap. Good quality photographs before and after surgery will help assess the results in a better way.'

'What should the surgeon do if he realizes he has messed up the surgery?'

'One can solve the problem with a touch up surgery. The surgeon should do some soul searching to find out what went wrong and maybe come to Dr. Vidur for training!'

Losing My Sovereignty

After a year, I automatically got promoted as a second year resident. While I was in the doctor's duty room, a ravishing girl entered.

'Sir, I am Nandini. I just joined as junior resident.'

I could not believe my luck. She had been posted with me. Nandini looked to be from the Northeast. Her features were a harmonious blend of Mongoloid and Caucasoid. Her velvety skin looked as if it could be marred by a touch.

'Nandini, where are you from?'

'Sir, I have done my MBBS from Dibrugarh Medical College.'

'I am sure your time here will be valuable,' I said and set about teaching her the basics of patient care.

The next day, she appeared in figure hugging jeans. My eyes hurt from spending too much time peeking at her from their corners.

'God, if you grant me this girl, I would not ask you for anything else,' I mumbled.

Then, my rationality asserted itself. It was highly unlikely that the girl who could stop traffic would have gone through five-and-a-half years of MBBS without hooking up with a guy. It was rude to directly ask her whether she was in a relationship or not.

Gradually, I reconciled myself to admiring her from a distance. God was playing tricks on me, again. A carrot was being dangled in front of me, but pulled back when I tried to grab it. My libido was persistent. It was obvious that I would have to eat my words and look for brides through the matrimonial columns.

Another uneventful week passed. During that time, I noticed that she was always on time and also put her heart and soul into patient care. My infatuation increased exponentially.

One Sunday, both of us were posted on emergency duty together. I was there for twenty-four hours. But, Nandini was supposed to be relieved at 8.00 p.m. by another junior resident, Saurabh. However, there wasn't any sign of him even at 8.30 p.m.

'Do not worry, sir. If he does not turn up, I will carry on till morning. There are so many pending tasks,' she said and started working.

Saurabh finally appeared at 9.00 p.m. 'I am sorry, sir. My bike broke down so I had to walk a long distance,' he quickly explained.

'Standard excuse,' I interrupted

'Boss, for once, I am speaking the truth! Look.'

He showed me his grease-smeared hands.

'Better maintain your crappy bike well. There are so many lives at stake here.'

'Right, sir.'

'Bye sir, I am leaving now,' Nandini said on seeing Saurabh.

'Thanks Nandini. Appreciated.'

The following Monday, a case of multiple facial fractures was admitted in emergency. After instructing Nandini to manage the ward, I went to the operation theatre. A young boy had his face smashed in a high speed car accident. Realigning the fractured bones with the help of mini-plates and stitching up the face took about seven hours.

When I came out of the operation theatre, it was 11.00 p.m. As long as I was engrossed in surgery, hunger and fatigue had taken a backseat. But afterwards, I felt as starved as someone undergoing a *genuine* fast unto death. My muscles and joints had also been abused during the last few hours. After leaving the operation theatre, I realized that the time for dinner at the cafeteria was over.

As I entered the duty room, Nandini greeted me with a smile. 'Sir, I am inspired by the way you managed the case. It must have been extremely taxing,' she said.

'As long as pretty girls like you are on duty, we remain charged up!' I said with a wink.

She must have been shocked because I had always maintained the façade of a drab scholar.

'I had guessed that you'd be starving and would make a meal of me! So along with my dinner, I ordered a plate for you as well,' she said.

My fatigue vanished in a flash.

'Thanks a lot.'

I sensed she had feelings for me. But before we could interact more, urgent work pushed us into different wards.

The next morning I was off duty for about four hours. I went to my room for a nap. There wasn't any possibility of sleep as I couldn't get my mind off Nandini. However, there was a complication. Her next posting was with Venkat. After racking my brain, I came up with a wicked plan – to exchange Venkat's duties with mine.

I told him that I needed the post duty offs to visit my relatives for marriage ceremonies. Venkat agreed to my request and looked pleased at being spared from doing nights. So, I got an extension of four days to bring about a critical surge in Nandini's love hormones.

On Thursday, both of us were together. I requested her to accompany me to the cafeteria. To my intense delight, she readily agreed, as if she had been eagerly awaiting it.

I played it safe with the typical conversation starters.

'So, where do your parents live?'

'I am from Tinsukia,' she replied.

'I think it is a town on the eastern end of Assam.'

'How do you know so much about my state?'

She looked startled.

'Well, I enjoy reading up on history and geography. I am particularly fascinated by the Northeast as I've never had the chance to visit it,' I replied.

Actually, I had spent the previous evening in the Book Browser Library looking up the history and geography of Assam. But that was just a small effort for the monumental reward at stake.

She looked at me intently and said, 'Sir, tell me something about your roots.'

'My roots are jumbled. My ancestral lands have been left in Pakistan after the Partition. I speak Punjabi at home but Hindi and English outside. To get over the confusion, I have started identifying myself as an Indian first.'

'What is your first love?' she asked.

'I will start in descending order. My third love is astronomy and second love is plastic surgery. Why don't you make a guess about the first one?'

Nandini rested her chin on her palm. After pondering for a while, she said, 'I am getting a few ideas.'

She paused again and then said, 'I give up. Now just reveal it to me quickly because I am dying to hear it.'

'Actually, that was a tough one for you. There is a vacancy for my first love and only a girl as sweet as honey could fit into the slot.'

'I hope you find her soon!'

For a second, I thought I was moving too fast. But Nandini seemed to be at ease. The conversation stopped for a while and I gazed intently into her eyes. But she lowered them.

'Sir, we should hurry back to the wards. There is a lot of work to be done,' she said firmly.

It seemed that her heart was not yet romantic enough to subdue her pragmatic mind.

The next day, again we bumped into each other at the cafeteria. She was chatting with a guy who looked to be Assamese.

'Hi sir, this is Paresh. He is from my medical college,' she said, after rising from her chair.

'Hi, please do carry on. I have a page from the ward.'

I smiled wryly and rushed off.

Actually, I was stumped because the chap could have been her boyfriend.

Two days later, we had our last common duty in the roster. There was a steady stream of casualties. So we didn't have any time to sit together. The seduction had hit a roadblock. In the morning, Nandini entered the duty room. She looked alert and fresh, even after being on her toes the entire night.

'I have finished all the work, sir. Taken the rounds, carried out your orders and completed the notes,' she said.

'Nandini, you are leaving the unit. But we have much left to discuss,' I said, in a shaky voice.

'Sir, you could come to my room. I hope you are free on Sunday evening.'

'Sure. Even if God calls me at that time, I would prefer your room. See you,' I said.

My joy knew no bounds. In a role reversal, Nandini had turned into the schemer. Obviously, amour was tightening its hold on her, too!

On Saturday, I called my cousin Sameer over and asked him to help me get some clothes.

'Dhruv, your clothes are awfully out of date. Make a bonfire of all these pleated trousers!'

'It is ironic that while my patients want to carry off body hugging jeans, I am expected to look like I'm from the sixties. But, I do need some casual wear for after work hours,' I said.

We came back from the market with a lot of trendy stuff. My cousin not only chipped in with his time but his wallet became lighter, too. I had to borrow money from him as I could have only bought the accessories by myself!

After spending a full hour getting ready, I made my way to Nandini's room. Single lady doctors, including Nandini, were given rooms on the top floor. Luckily, there wasn't any bar on visitors. The girls were obviously thought to be mature enough to weed out the bad boys.

Nandini looked the prettiest I had ever seen her. Her lips and eyes stood out. That day, both of us were free from hospital pressure. So we talked non-stop for hours on subjects from the sublime to the frivolous.

She began, 'I have fond memories of my childhood. Since I was five, I have stayed in a boarding school in Guwahati. Despite the strictness, it was a lot of fun.'

'What is your favourite sport?' I asked.

Actually, I was trying to gauge how her figure had become so pleasantly curvy.

'I used to play badminton and handball regularly. But I have gained weight after shifting to Delhi, because I am not exercising much.'

'But you are putting on weight only in the right places!' I said, as I shamelessly stared at her assets.

'Shut up, Dhruv!' she shouted.

I liked the way she had called me by my first name. The end of the formality was a good sign for our relationship.

I tried to change the topic.

'By the way, are you friends with Paresh?'

'Oh! That guy is a harmless character. He got married two months ago. We were just discussing the problems we face in Delhi,' she smiled.

She continued, 'Now tell me your secrets.'

'To tell you the truth, I have had friendships with a couple of girls during my MBBS and MS days, but none that could be called true love.'

My score was not very high. But I still lied to her because I did not want to risk putting her off.

'Your story is so similar to mine. Well, I was also friendly with a few boys in medical college, but no Romeo and Juliet story. When I joined the medical college, I was given a list of rules by my parents, the main one being to avoid affairs.'

'So did you do as instructed? It is said that you grow up the day you stop following all of your parents' diktats.'

'I did as they told me because I could not have hurt them. After I finished MBBS, my parents started looking for a match for me. Dad made it as tough as an I.I.T. entrance exam. Predictably, none of the prospective grooms got past the initial round. In frustration, Dad taunted me that I should have found someone suitable by myself during the MBBS course only. I reminded him that he was contradicting his own rule which restricted me from mixing with the boys!'

'Good for me though. Your walls came down at the right moment. That reminds me of my sister's matrimonial process. Dad insisted that the boy should not be a teetotaler. He wanted a son-in-law with whom he could bond over drinks.'

Suddenly, we noticed it had turned dark.

'I think it's time to say goodbye.' She daintily reminded me I had overstayed my time in her room.

'Okay, I'll take your leave then. But I do look forward to a nice evening on Saturday. How about dinner at Connaught Place?'

'I wouldn't be comfortable with that.'

'Please! Please!' I pestered her like an obstinate child.

She thought for a while and then said, 'All right. I will come, but on one condition.'

'What now?'

'Nothing complicated. From now on, I want to call you by your first name.'

'Done. But, in the hospital, you will have to address me as "sir" only. There, I will also retain the right to yell at you and call you inefficient and a dud!'

'If you scold me in the wards, I will settle the score with you later.'

When I held her soft hand for a parting handshake, I was extremely turned on.

The next day, I was in a great mood and was very happy with my life; I was even singing love songs. There were a lot of cases to be worked on and shown to the chief. During the afternoon, Venkat and I were having our usual hurried lunch.

'So, how far have you gone with Nandini?' Venkat asked with a wry smile.

It was obvious that I had been spotted in Nandini's room by somebody. Gossip seemed to be moving faster than light!

'Venkat, we just enjoy each other's company. That's all.'

We were joined by our senior Nayan.

He said, 'Hats off to you for bedding the smoking hot chick!'

I kept silent. There was no point in giving an explanation to the lecher who looked at all women as sexual objects.

The next day, the chief had to take detailed rounds in the wards. Since morning, all the doctors and nurses had been on their toes to keep his wrath at bay. But from the very beginning, his focus was on me.

After I failed to answer a question, he addressed all the doctors on the round, including Nandini, 'Today, I have made a new discovery. Dr. Dhruv has been evolving backwards. If he continues to regress, he will gradually develop a tail and make his home at the top of a tree in the hospital campus!'

I felt worse than an ape as I couldn't even hide or escape.

In the next bed, a patient who had undergone a skin grafting operation was due for discharge.

I told the chief, 'The wound is almost healed. The patient wants to go home because one of his relatives, who is a registered medical practitioner in the village, has volunteered to do further dressings.'

'Go ahead. Undoubtedly, the village doctor will give better care than you!' the chief replied.

I felt like I was being flogged in a public square in a medieval town. One of the chief's cronies had probably spilled the beans about Nandini and me.

'It seems that the old man has a crush on her, which automatically makes me his enemy. That is why he is resorting to these cheap tactics,' I said to myself.

After the rounds, I finished my work and rushed to my room. After a few minutes, there was a knock. My irritation at being disturbed vanished when I found that it was Nandini at the door.

'What a surprise! Come in.'

'I felt like talking to you because you must be quite upset.'

'I am not as dim-witted as the chief tried to prove today. He was just targeting me.'

'That was obvious. Now cheer up. The best way for us to get even with the chief is to become closer! I will see you for dinner tomorrow. I am going…don't want to be late for my duty. Bye.'

Nandini rushed out of my room.

My worst fears were confirmed the next morning when I was called to the chief's office. I entered with a morose expression on my face.

The chief said, 'I do not want to interfere in your personal life. But you must understand that an affair with your immediate junior at the workplace causes distractions. Other junior residents will presume that you will favour Nandini. A hospital is a place for treating the sick, not for hanky-panky.'

Having been cornered, the only way out was dead cat bounce.

I spoke like a belligerent defendant pleading to a judge.

'Sir, the resident doctors are mostly busy in the wards; there is hardly any social life outside this hospital. Courtship should be allowed in the hospital grounds! Both of us want to be together, with your blessing. If you post us in different units, there will be no issues regarding the work.'

The chief's stern face turned serene and then joyous.

'You did a lot of overacting, but were able to convey your point nonetheless. Nandini is the most hardworking doctor amongst the junior residents. She can take good care of a donkey like you! But there should be no romancing in the wards.'

You did not have to be a psychologist to judge that the chief liked Nandini. 'Thank you sir, thank you so much.'

I rushed out of the office.

Since almost everyone had come to know about us, Nandini and I could go out together openly. But that took away the thrill of clandestine meetings. Nandini kept her promise to accompany me on a special evening.

I entered her room to escort her. I was seeing her in a skirt for the first time. Her midi was just the right length, making her look elegant while standing and sensual while sitting. Hints of a floral scent from her perfume enchanted me. We started for the inner circle of Connaught Place.

Inside the Red Dragon Restaurant, we were lucky to get a nice, secluded table.

'You told me that nobody knew about our friendship. But, since yesterday, many nurses and doctors have been asking me what's going on,' she said.

'I swear, I never talked about us to anybody, not even to Venkat, when I exchanged my duties with him. Maybe someone spotted me going to your room.'

'Cheater! You changed your on-call dates with Venkat so that you had all the time in the world to impress me. I also wondered why we had so many duties together,' she said.

'Look, Nandini. I am not one of those super smart guys who take just a few minutes to make a girl go weak in the knees. So I needed a lot of interaction with you,' I replied.

After a couple of drinks, both of us relaxed. The limbic system, the area of the brain responsible for emotions, became active and sentimentality came to the fore.

I asked, 'What do you like the most about me?'

'I think it would be your mature conversations. Most of the boys here behave in a childish manner.'

'What else?'

I was hungry for more.

'Your long nose and naughty smile.'

We were having a heart to heart but neither of us had said the magical four letter word.

'Why are you so desperate to trap me?' she asked.

'I like the whole package. Should I start from the top or from below?'

She said, 'Shut up! All guys have a tunnel vision, focused on the body.'

'Okay, the best thing I like about you is your dedication to your work,' I said.

We started for our hostel past midnight. As soon as I bolted the car door, her perfume began to turn me on. She looked surreal in the dim lighting. The car had covered just about a kilometre when I felt powerless to overrule my primal instincts. Looking for a dark spot, I came across a stretch where there wasn't a street light. I profusely thanked the municipal corporation for its inefficiency! Moving the car to the left, I stopped under a tree. After turning my gaze towards her, I put my arms around her and pulled her towards me. I pouted in anticipation of locking my lips with hers.

The unthinkable happened in a split second. Nandini pushed me away.

'How dare you violate me! We have been seeing each other for just three weeks. You haven't even confessed your love for me. You're a typical North Indian male chauvinist,' she fumed.

I had never imagined that she could become so hopping mad.

Shifting to damage control mode, I said, 'Nandini, I am so sorry. I lost my cool in the heat of the moment.'

'Just leave me alone,' she said scornfully.

There was a ghastly silence in the car during the rest of the journey. As soon as we reached the hostel, she rushed towards her room, without even looking back.

I regretted hurting her feelings. But there was a contradiction in her rebuttal. Even though we had not said it to each other, both of us were actually in love. So, what was wrong in expressing my affection with a kiss.

The next day, I reached the departmental office ten minutes before the morning attendance.

As soon as I saw Nandini, I said, 'Good morning.'

Nandini repeated the same coldly. She quickly moved on without even looking at me, as if a queen was passing a slave in her palace. It was the same for the next three days. She was prolonging my agony to a breaking point.

But, I persisted. On the fifth morning, the fog began to dissipate. She replied to my greeting with a smile. I knew it was just a matter of time before things went back to normal. The same evening, she made a visit to my room.

'Dhruv! We need to talk.'

We decided to go to the Indian Coffee House. It was 31st July and I was almost broke. So, a trendy restaurant was out of the question.

That day, I was treading very cautiously.

'Dhruv, I am sorry for overreacting the last time. I hope you are not angry,' she said.

'Not at all.'

'So, when are you taking me out?' she blushed.

'Tomorrow. Both of us will be free and I'll be getting my pay cheque as well.'

'Done.'

The time was right to tell her how I felt.

Just before dinner, I had butterflies in my stomach as I was working on the words she was dying to hear.

We entered Pakwan, an Indian restaurant with dim lighting. As soon as we were seated, I blurted out, 'Nandini, I love you from the bottom of my heart and want to spend the rest of my life with you.'

Instead of looking dreamy and misty-eyed, she started grinning.

'Come on, Dhruv! I felt like an examiner listening to a candidate. Take a deep breath and say it again.'

I looked into her eyes, gestured with my hands, and said the words again with confidence.

'I love you, too.'

'Something is missing from your side,' I said.

'You mean marrying you? I will have to think about whether you are marriage material.'

'Why strain yourself unnecessarily. All the points are in my favour. A decent guy with only good addictions, like Nandini! Of course, it's another matter if you look at me as mere time pass.'

'Silly, I have been dreaming of being Mrs Khanna ever since I fell for you. A lady can judge a male doctor by how he treats his patients. You did well in that test.'

'Okay, then let us talk business. To convince your parents, you may have to indulge in some cheap histrionics like saying, "I will kill myself if you take Dhruv away from me", and so on. As for my parents, there is no need for their consent. Rather, they will heave a big sigh of relief when they come to know about my marriage plans.'

'To tell you the truth, my father is already on a matrimonial hunt. He has shortlisted some boys from our community in Assam. So, to get approval for a North Indian boy, and that too a *Punju*, will not be easy.'

As we sat in the car on our return, I put all my carnal desires under the command of the principled section of the brain. We were about halfway to our hostel when I felt a warm breath on my left ear.

She whispered, 'Dhruv, can I hold your hand?'

It was a pleasant surprise, but from then on, she controlled me like a puppeteer. I gave my left hand to her. She told me to stop the car on the side of the road and locked her lips with mine.

The first feeling of her luscious lips is still fresh in my mind. After we had kissed for a while, she grabbed my hair and bit my lower lip. She then pushed my head back and told me to drive.

'This was just a teaser; the main course will come only after marriage.'

I drove back happy with dishevelled hair and a swollen lower lip! Once her passion had erupted, it surpassed the fieriness of the Bhut Jholakia chilli. I was aroused by the mere thought of having all of her to myself.

The next day, I asked her, 'Sweetie, how was it yesterday?'

'Beyond words. I have not washed my face since I kissed you, because I don't want to lose the taste of your lips!'

The day after that I went home and told my parents about Nandini.

'He could not find a suitable match in the whole of Delhi. Will a girl from Assam adjust in our family?' Dad said cynically.

'Nowadays it is the elders who have to adjust to their daughters-in-law! After being so desperate for him to marry, why are you questioning his choice?' Mom interrupted.

'Just meet her once. I am sure you will give me thumbs up right away,' I said.

Moving swiftly, I brought Nandini home.

Later, Mom told me, 'You took your time, but seem to have hit the jackpot.'

'So, how do you feel about my parents?' I asked Nandini.

'Your mom is sweet. Your dad doesn't talk much, but has a great sense of humour.'

'Did you have a word with your parents?'

'It is all clear at my end. Two days ago, I rang up Papa. As expected, he was puzzled at first. But I told him all about you, just the good qualities, of course! This morning, I got his approval. But he needs to meet you and your family before the final decision.'

After a week, Nandini's parents reached Delhi. Her father came across as an affable person. Her mother, a teacher, bonded well with Mom. It was clear that our values were similar, despite the cultural differences. The middle class is the same everywhere!

We got the green signal all the way. The wedding was fixed for ten days later. For our honeymoon, we planned to visit Assam so I could visit her home and meet the relatives who couldn't make it to the wedding.

A small banquet hall was booked as only close family members and friends were invited. The next day, I told the chief about my wedding plans. He hugged me for the first time.

'You are literally milking the department by getting a degree as well as a charming wife!'

'Only with your blessings.'

'You get a leave for twelve-days. Go ahead and enjoy yourself.'

The chief had been extra generous. A twelve-day leave for a resident doctor was great luxury. Later, I announced the news in my ward. It was transmitted quickly to the whole department.

My sister reached just one day before the wedding. She and Nandini spent an hour together.

It was smooth sailing on the day of the wedding. The extended families were introduced to each other. The Assamese guests danced to the beats of the *dhol* as energetically as everyone else.

After breezing through the ceremonies and chants, we finally experienced the much awaited moment of togetherness in the honeymoon suite of Shiraz Hotel. As our bodies came together, our chemistry elevated the union into what seemed like a celestial celebration.

As we were getting ready to leave the hotel in the evening, I asked her, 'Doll, how was it?'

Nandini blushed and replied, 'Mind blowing! As they say, the first time is the best.'

The (Not So) Glorious Profession

During our honeymoon, we discovered a lot about each other that we liked. However, differences also came to surface. But, the fights were friendly and compensated by the fun of reconciliation.

Our first home was a cramped hostel room which served as a living room, bedroom, storeroom, kitchen and at times, as a guest room! Whenever I had emergency duty, I made it a point to visit her two or three times.

I tried to initiate Nandini into astronomy, so we could add variety to our nightlife. Initially, she participated enthusiastically, but her curiosity soon waned. Then, there was talk about an astronomy event which excited everyone. A meteor shower was due in a few days. I felt it was worth showing the spectacle to Nandini.

On the night of the event, we drove down to a pitch dark area near the Surajkund Lake on the Delhi-Haryana border. When we reached the vantage point, I was surprised to see a number of vehicles already parked there. Apart from sky watchers, there were people who had probably come to wish on the shooting stars.

After watching the sky, I felt a bit uneasy. Only the brightest of stars were visible. The smog of the megalopolis had invaded the outskirts as well. My worst fears came true as I saw just a couple of meteors in an hour. There was no sign of fireworks like display of shooting stars across the night sky.

I was dejected.

A teenage boy, standing nearby, said to his father, 'Dad, all we will get from the sky is a shower of paper slips with "April fool" written over them!'

All the grim people around him burst into laughter, and on that note, we all returned home.

As I was grappling with a bulky textbook in the hostel room the next day, Nandini came running in and hugged me tightly.

'So, are we going to be a trio soon?' I asked the usual question.

'There are other things to be excited about apart from babies. I cracked the Assam state postgraduate entrance test with a rank of 137. I'll be able to get my MD in a clinical subject,' she said excitedly.

But I wasn't enthusiastic.

'Congrats. I am really happy for you. Every doctor aspires to do a post graduation and I would be the last person to get in the way of your career. But thinking of living without you for the next three years is making me jittery,' I said.

'Without your shoulder to lean on, it would be as tough for me too. But getting into an MD is as difficult as finding a husband like you!'

Then, Nandini took me in her arms and continued, 'Physical separation is only going to make our bond stronger. We'll be in touch regularly and of course dreaming about each other every day and night.'

'But, we won't be able to have a baby during this time,' I said.

Nandini turned pensive. After a while, she said, 'Dhruv, family life is as dear to me as my career. What should I do?'

My plain speaking seemed to have made her think twice. She was probably aware of the unwritten rule that female doctors weren't supposed to get pregnant while doing their MD.

I kept on cerebrating till late at night. By next evening, I had reconciled myself to the idea.

I told her, 'Go ahead and join without any guilt. God willing, we have our whole future to spend together.'

'Thank you for your support and trust.'

Her moist eyes said it all.

'Thank you for considering me too as trustworthy,' I replied.

Three days after she left for Delhi, I got the much-awaited phone call from her.

'Hey! I got my MD in paediatrics, my favourite subject. I'll have to join Dibrugarh Medical College within a week.'

After a few days, I received the first letter from her. Her sentimental words made me so emotional that I replied with an even bigger tear-jerker! Writing to each other opened up the deepest recesses of our minds.

Meanwhile, the chief began delegating work to me. It was a sign that he had developed enough confidence in me. I had to operate on cases independently and make the juniors operate under my supervision. But power came at a price! I was now accountable for my juniors as well. Unfortunately, some of them seemed to be hell bent on reinforcing the idiom, 'To err is human!'

Three months after my marriage, I was posted to Dr. Salil's unit. The first case on the operative list was a three-month-old boy. Due to a birth defect, called cleft lip, his upper lip was vertically split on one side. I was disturbed as I noticed the big kohl mark on his forehead that his mother had put there. Although the cute child was in the danger zone, the doctors were not likely to cast an evil eye on him.

Dr. Anita, the senior anaesthesiologist, took charge. The monitors started making their jarring noise. All the injections for induction of anaesthesia had been filled and labelled.

As soon as the first injection was given, the unthinkable happened. A cacophony of alarms from the monitors filled the operation theatre. The flat wave on the E.C.G. monitor was the sign of a cardiac arrest.

Everyone swung into frenzied action. Resuscitation injections were tossed around and immediately given. An endotracheal tube was inserted through the air passage. D.C. shock was also given. But we seemed to be running out of luck. Nothing was working.

'Dhruv! Inform the relatives that his condition is critical,' Dr. Salil instructed me.

On reaching the waiting area outside the operation theatre, I came across the usual scene. Groups of people were anxiously waiting for their loved ones to come out safe and sound. Some were praying, but most were de-stressing by gossiping about other relatives.

'Who is with Mridul?' I asked loudly.

Immediately, the child's parents and relatives surrounded me.

'Your child had an unusual reaction to an injection. He is in a serious condition, but all efforts are being made for his recovery.'

All of them folded their hands. To my embarrassment, the father of the child prostrated himself at my feet and said, 'Please save my child at any cost.'

I went inside the operation theatre. The situation was the same. After another fifteen minutes of resuscitation, the child was declared dead.

There was an eerie silence in the operation theatre. Even the masks could not conceal everyone's shame and horror. There was also the fear of how the relatives would react. Dr. Anita's three-decade-old reputation of being a safe anaesthesiologist had been blown to smithereens.

Dr. Salil said to me, 'Inform the chief about the mortality.' I rushed to meet the chief.

'Sir, an infant with a cleft lip died on the operation table.'

The chief was dumbfounded as well, but he soon composed himself.

'The operative as well as the anaesthesia team is second to none. I am sure there has been no negligence. It was most likely an unusually severe reaction to the relaxant injection that occurs on rare occasions, in one out of a thousand cases. But, this child is not just a statistic. For his family, the loss is nothing short of a catastrophe. Anyway, inform the relatives of the facts as they happened.'

So, the multitasking resident doctor also had to act as the messenger of death. I went to the waiting area again. The relatives mobbed me.

'I am sorry. Your child is no more. We did everything we could, but his heart did not start again,' I conveyed calmly.

The father of the child almost collapsed and had to be given support. Soon, the wails of the female relatives started resonating through the department. Some of them started beating their breasts. I rushed back to the theatre as there were a lot of notes and death forms to be completed.

After about an hour, I came out of the operation theatre. There was a lot of noise that seemed to be coming from outside the front entrance. When I walked on, I saw a crowd. They were undoubtedly the agitated relatives of the deceased child. I rushed downstairs.

'*Kutte doctor haye haye!*'

A slogan that equated doctors with dogs was being repeated. A few brickbats shattered the front window glass.

The crowd began chanting, '*Doctor khooni hain* - Doctors are killers.'

An old lady, with countless wrinkles on her face, shouted at the top of her voice, '*Tum sab doctor keede pad ke maro!*'

She was wishing that all the doctors who had treated the child would die a slow death.

The few policemen at the hospital were vastly outnumbered by the mob and were hesitant to use force. They were securing the entrance to the department while waiting for reinforcements to arrive. Sensing danger, some of the doctors and staff quietly slipped out of harm's way through a back exit. The chief appeared on the scene. But, to our dismay, he moved towards the entrance.

'Sir, please avoid direct contact with them until more policemen get here,' a horrified Dr. Mohan said to him.

'Don't worry, I am not going into the mob,' the chief replied confidently, like a brash commander.

'It seems that senility has finally caught up with him. His heroics may put him at real risk of getting roughed up by the mob,' Venkat said.

The others seemed to agree with him. As soon as the chief reached the main entrance, a few policemen formed a protective circle around him. A burly man, who was commanding the crowd, rushed forward with a few others. Some of the doctors closed their eyes. But, to our utter surprise, the men bowed in front of the chief and touched his feet. He conversed with them for a couple of minutes. Then, the ringleader addressed the crowd and soon most of the people, except the close relatives of the child, dispersed.

Like sheep trailing a herder, all of us followed the chief into his office. We were curious to know how he managed to calm the enraged crowd so quickly.

'After looking through my office window, I identified the leader of the mob, Shishpal. Just a year ago, I had saved his son's life by operating upon the child at midnight. He required an urgent blood transfusion the next day. Since his blood group, AB negative, wasn't available, I donated blood for him. So, I was confident that on seeing me, he would be pacified. I explained the situation to them. Shishpal told everybody that since I had gone out of my way to save his child's life, no efforts must have been spared for the deceased child,' the chief said.

Although the situation had been salvaged in the nick of time, the events of that day could not be erased from my mind. It was the first time I saw ordinary people turn into a mob. As if the risk of contracting tuberculosis, hepatitis and AIDS wasn't enough, there were irate relatives waiting to beat me up. I called the medical profession a third-rate profession. Sleep brought no succour as nightmares tormented me further.

I started my work in the department the next day, but my heart wasn't in it. In the afternoon, the chief called me to his office to give me instructions about a patient.

'Dhruv, it seems like you still haven't got over yesterday's events,' the chief said.

His experienced eye had read my face and guessed the deadlock in my mind.

'Sir, even after working dedicatedly for donkey's years in the hospital, I could be called a murderer and possibly assaulted for an act of God.'

'See, we Indians have wild mood swings. When the Indian cricket team performs badly, the public goes to the extent of burning effigies of the star players. The relatives had an irrational but firm belief that the wrong injection had been given to the child. So they refused to buy your explanations.'

'Have you ever faced a similar situation before?'

'I've had a number of complications too, but most patients have taken them as the will of God. Still, I have had close shaves with agitated relatives. When you drive a lot, once in a while you might have a mishap. This does not mean that we stop driving. Do not forget that often, doctors do make a blunder but get away with it by sweeping it under the rug.'

'I do agree that patients are often wronged.'

'There is a saying that during the examination of a patient, a few doctors palpate their wallets too! A person, who has been a victim of malpractice, starts harbouring suspicions about the medical community as a whole.'

I interrupted the chief to defend my fraternity. 'On the other hand, even if a patient dies of a critical illness, the patients' relatives often stage demonstrations just to avoid paying the bills.'

'True. In our materialistic society, the sacred doctor-patient relationship has disintegrated. That is the root cause for the increase of litigations and conflicts.'

His words did assuage me to some extent.

But my hands still trembled during surgeries. I saw all the patients' relatives as potential trouble makers. Dr. Salil himself seemed to be devastated. The flamboyant doctor didn't shave for days. He confessed to me that he had taken antidepressant pills for two weeks.

I slowly regained my composure as the impact of the incident started to become fainter. Then, I was caressed by a gust of cool mountain breeze. Nandini announced that she was coming for a week-long stay.

Before Nandini's arrival, I brought some semblance of order to my chaotic hostel room. As soon as she got down from the train, we hugged each other tightly, oblivious of the crowds around us. On reaching home, I pounced on her like a hungry wolf.

'Come on, Dhruv, I'm here for a week,' she whispered. Brushing aside her feeble and phony protest, I shut her up with my lips and our bodies did the talking after that.

Over dinner, I told her about my close shave with the mob following the death of a child on the operation table. I expected her to sympathize. However, she was more perturbed over the loss of a young life.

'So, how are things at your end?' I asked her.

'Oh dear! It is so tough...but I have gradually started enjoying it. A few days ago, the chief was doing the morning rounds. And a mother complained that her child had been crying for almost an hour during the night. I was sternly instructed that I had no right to sleep even for a minute when a child had been this restless. This is the standard of care that's expected from us. Post night duty, we get off for just about four hours. But, the clinical experience and teaching is great.'

After a few days, she left me high and dry yet again. As I was about to complete my residency tenure, the countdown to the M.Ch. exam began. I had to pass it in the first attempt or face a sentence of six more months in the department. Horror stories of previous examinations, told by the seniors, made it look like an attempt to conquer Mount K2. However, according to Dr. Vidur, passing the M.Ch. had never been easier.

'In our times, multiple attempts were the norm. There were a number of instances when the candidate had to marry the daughter of the boss to pass!'

A month before the exam, I turned into a bookworm. But I had an unexpected interlude. One morning, while I was in the ward, I received a visitor I had sworn never to meet in my life, again. However, Manika was all smiles and we strolled to the cafeteria.

'Manika, we promised never to see each other again.'

'It was you who vowed not to meet me, but forgot to say that I couldn't meet you! So, I can come to you whenever I please.'

She was a veteran at making my anger disappear.

'Smart girl! No wonder you have always been one up on me.'

'But I am regretting it now. This is my first visit to India after shifting to the US. I am flying back tomorrow. The trip seemed incomplete without seeing you.'

'How are you doing? You must be enjoying life in California.'

'Everything is all right from the outside. I've cleared the Foreign Graduates Entrance test and have started my residency. Rajat has got a good job. We live in a nice suburban home in Orange County. But the spark in our marriage is missing. Remember, you used to call arranged marriages a farce? I realize it is true now.'

I felt sorry for her, but liked the way she confided in me.

After a brief lull, the exam fever besieged me again. Dr. Dwivedi was likely to be one of the external examiners, again.

My senior Nayan told me, 'Last year, the candidate's performance was border line. The internal examiners had requested the external examiners to clear Deepak as he was a good worker. However, Dr. Dwivedi put his foot down. He reasoned that an improperly trained doctor was a danger to the society. The guy was in tears but gradually composed himself with the support of his seniors. He passed in the next attempt.'

On the day of the exam, I took a couple of antacid tablets and reached the examination venue in a crisp white coat. My mental third degree torture was to last for two whole days. Since there were just two examinees, the chances of the examiners being inattentive were minimal.

Waiting outside the chief's office, I heard loud laughter from inside. The examiners were cracking jokes and enjoying themselves. When my name was called, I rushed inside and bowed my head so far down that I could see the wall from between my legs. In addition to that, I made such a pitiable face as if a supermodel had just broken up with me!

'Have a seat,' Dr. Adarsh said.

'Which sub-speciality of plastic surgery are you interested in?' Dr Dwivedi, asked me.

'Sir, my favourite sub-speciality is cosmetic surgery.'

It was better to reveal one's pet subject honestly because more questions were likely to be asked from it.

'So, you're interested in a branch you can mint money in!' Dr. Dwivedi asked.

'Yes. I want a good lifestyle with lots of fame! But I will always follow medical ethics.'

I still don't recall how I gathered the courage to say that.

'Good. I appreciate your honesty. All the best.'

I was given a few cases to prepare for the presentations. The patients seemed to be amused by my shakiness and some even wished me good luck. Then, my viva started. Being no match for the veterans, I was caught on the wrong foot during some questions.

On the second day, my performance was better, though the examiners tried their best to distract me. I had been coached by the seniors; the examiner is always right. So, I never argued even if an answer that was right according to me was pointed out to be wrong.

Venkat and I were made to wait outside the office while the examiners enjoyed their coffee. Finally, after about fifteen minutes that felt like fifteen hours to us, we were called in. I was dismayed to see grumpy faces. The few minor mistakes we had committed were pointed out as colossal blunders.

'Both of you are through. Go and enjoy yourselves,' the chief said with a gesture.

As I instinctively rushed to touch his feet, he hugged me and the other examiners patted me on the back too.

Next day, I went to meet the chief to thank him.

'Congratulations, you did very well in the exam. In fact, the examiners have suggested we keep you in the department,' the chief said.

'Sir, I am twenty-nine years of age. For the last eleven years, my parents have been supporting me. It's high time I stood on my own feet. I would like to work here for the time being. But, kindly relieve me if I find a better opportunity.'

'After getting through the exam, you are free from our clutches. So, there is no choice but to say that I agree to all your terms and conditions,' the chief said sarcastically.

'Sir, please don't take offence. You will always be my guru,' I said as I touched his feet.

To my surprise, he even invited me over to his house for tea.

I made my way to chief's bungalow in Vasant Vihar and was welcomed like a first time visitor.

'So, you must be the boss at home, too.' I deliberately put up this question to the chief in the presence of his better half, to initiate some spicy conversation.

'Boss! No way. Mohini thinks I am a workaholic who neglects his family. My daughters think of me as a relic from the stone age just because I cannot speak English with a posh accent!'

'He is exaggerating, but only a bit!' said Dr. Mohini, his gynaecologist wife.

'This is the story of every house. The generation gap has deepened and has become a chasm,' I commented.

'The message is...that promotions at the workplace often lead to demotions at home! ' the chief said.

As I left his house, I realized that the chief had become more friendly than bossy. With the burden of the post doctoral course gone, I could breathe easily. But like any other human mind, mine invented problems. I now started worrying about my future.

A Working Holiday

A few months after joining as a senior resident, I attended an international conference on plastic surgery in Mumbai. The legends of plastic surgery from all over the world had congregated there. I sensed an opportunity to find a mentor from a country where plastic surgery was commonplace. This way I could sharpen my less practiced skills.

During the lunch break, a local plastic surgeon, Dr. Ketan, pointed towards a corner and said, 'Look at that chap with the grey suit and blue tie. Dr. Gregory Palmer from Chicago. You must have already heard a lot about him. The best thing about Dr. Palmer is that he encourages visiting fellows, especially Indians.'

The incredible coincidence that Chicago was my sister's hometown seemed unreal.

'Last year, I spent six months with Dr. Palmer and learnt a lot,' Ketan said.

'But why is he so friendly towards Indians?' I asked.

'He is an Indophile and visits us almost every year. After attending the conferences, he puts on khakis and tours different regions of our country.'

'May God create more creatures like him,' I said.

For a man of his stature, Dr. Palmer was extremely friendly by Indian standards. He had a square, handsome face with green eyes and unlike most Caucasians, he did not tower above us.

I introduced myself to him. The moment he came to know that I had done my plastic surgery degree from Arogyam Hospital, he readily agreed to take me on as a visiting fellow for three months. Dr. Palmer promised to send a letter addressed to the American Embassy from his office to me.

I called up Nandini and told her, 'I am going to be in the US for three months on a fellowship. It happened so fast I did not have the time to discuss it with you.'

Nandini seemed shocked.

After a long pause, she said, 'How will I keep tabs on you so you don't go astray?'

'You can sleep in peace. I will be staying with my sis in Chicago,' I replied.

'But your brother-in-law will ruin you. He might try to display his hospitality by showing you the sleazy side of Chicago.'

'If you are so on the edge, you can tell Bhavya to keep a check on me.'

'Just joking. I am sure you will heed the saying that is often written on the backs of trucks - *Dekhi jao par chhedna mat*. So, keep admiring pretty ladies, but do not touch!'

I received so much unsolicited advice about preparing for the visa interview at the American Embassy that I could have written a self help book! As coached, I reached the embassy before the crack of dawn. To my utter surprise, I found myself at the end of a long queue of people. After the visa proceedings began, I saw the successful ones come out with unbridled jubilation as if making it big in America was child's play. I remembered a saying my dad quoted a lot – 'A jackass from Lahore, will remain so in Peshawar!'

When I reached inside, the only wish on my mind was for the ordeal to end soon. The counsellor, a brunette, took just two minutes to grant me a single entry visa. But, she scowled all the while. She was probably cursing Dr. Palmer for leaving her hands tied when he had given me a personal invitation. As I came out of the Embassy and made the victory sign, my parents seemed to be even more jubilant than they had been at my birth!

The following day, I visited Dr. Vidur.

'I am sure I'll pick up quite a few things from you after your return. The trip will also be handy for you to impress your patients as a doctor trained in America!'

'Sir, you have spent a lot of time in the US. Any advice?'

'Pick up the good points and improvise them to suit Indian conditions.'

The chief graciously relieved me from the department. On my last day, as I walked back, a melange of memories flashed through my mind. It would be difficult to repay the place that had given me so much.

It was a usual late night boarding. While waiting in the terminal building, I imagined that Nandini had come to see me off with tears in her eyes. The boarding announcement interrupted my daydream. The flight was to stop at Heathrow, London before moving to Chicago.

After arriving at Chicago, I encountered a burly inspector at the immigration counter. He cleared my documents but made me feel unwelcome with his boorish conduct. I felt like taking the same flight back.

'Immigration staff is the same everywhere. This ignorant fool should visit India to see that not all Indians are fakirs sleeping on a bed of nails!' I murmured.

'Hope you had a comfortable journey,' Bhavya said, on receiving me at the arrival area.

'Oh, wonderful.'

I decided not to tell my sister about my humiliation at the airport so as to avoid upsetting the emotional fool.

Our car started eating up the miles after entering a freeway.

The suburban home had superb vistas all around, including a small lake with ducks. My fatigue dissipated soon as we gathered around the fireplace and caught up with each other.

'Just let me know if there is any particular activity on your wish list,' Bhavya said.

'I am dying to go to a meet of astronomy hobbyists.'

Agrim, my brother-in-law, began searching the net. He soon discovered an event that was going to be held two weeks later in the countryside, north of Chicago. The moonless night and the weekend were luckily coinciding. Both of them agreed to accompany me as they seemed eager to have a novel experience.

I explored the house and later strolled along the sidewalks of the block. Since there was no corner shop or tea stall in the neighbourhood, I could not catch up with the local gossip. In the evening, I went on a shopping binge at a superstore which was as big as an Indian *mohalla*.

My sister dropped me off at the hospital the next day. From then on, I was to stay at a nearby apartment and visit them only on weekends.

'Immerse yourself in plastic and cosmetic surgery. You will be compensated with lots of fun on the weekends.'

She left me after giving me this verbal boost.

The Lakeview Hospital was a cross between a resort and a hospital. True to its name, it had a splendid view of Lake

Michigan. Less intimidating than a normal multi-specialty hospital, it was a fitting place for plastic surgery.

Dr. Palmer welcomed me with a hug.

'Welcome gentleman. By the end of your tenure, you should be confident of performing all types of cosmetic and plastic surgery. Hopefully you will mould the faces of Bollywood divas once you get back.'

His frequent visits to India had seemingly got him hooked on to Hindi cinema.

'Thank you very much. But I live in the city of Delhi which is a thousand miles from Mumbai.'

'So what, you can always relocate. Changing cities, careers and girlfriends are essential for growth!'

I was sent to the secretary, Erika, who showed me around the department. Four American doctors were doing their residency there. International flavour was provided by the visiting fellows from Venezuela, Japan, Egypt and Poland. Their broken English reminded me of the British comedy, *Mind Your Language*.

The first day was spent in the outpatient department. Jack, an elderly man, made my day.

'Hey! Good to see you after a long time. What brings you here?' Dr. Palmer asked Jack, who was reclining on the examination chair.

'I thought that my old friend Dr. Palmer might be running short of money! So, I have come to share some of the fortune I inherited,' he said and left Dr. Palmer short of words.

'Okay, I want a revision of the facelift you performed fifteen years ago,' Jack came to the point.

'What is your motivation? You must be looking for a girlfriend to spend the rest of your money on!' Dr. Palmer said.

'I would not mind that windfall, either!'

Then, Dr. Palmer got down to serious business. He assessed Jack's wrinkles and jowls. After a clinical discussion with us, he made a plan and posted him for surgery to be performed the next day.

Later, Dr. Palmer told me, 'As you have seen, many patients make us happy with a humour that is uniquely American. But, there are a few unforgiving types too, who go for litigation.'

During the lunch break, I introduced myself to the chief resident, Michael Walters, a very big, blonde fellow.

'So, Michael, where were you previously?' I asked.

'You must be wondering why a person old enough to be a professor is working as a resident doctor. Actually, I joined medical school after working as an aeronautical engineer for around ten years.'

'Interesting. But why did you leave your engineering job?'

'I fell in love with Dr. Cynthia, who was posted in our company as medical officer and ended up marrying her. I gradually developed a fascination for medical science and the rest is history!'

'In India, if someone proposed such a switch, he would be called half mad!'

'I have not allowed the years I spent as an aeronautical engineer to go to waste. I am using my experience of designing helmets to devise a metallic apparatus for lengthening facial bones and fixing facial fractures. That will hopefully be a big leap forward for mankind.'

After the lunch break, the outpatient session started again. Next in line was Nancy, a lady in her early forties. She wanted her breasts augmented with implants. Dr. Palmer examined her thoroughly. Later, he asked Jenny, the attending nurse, to take her to the adjoining room and help her choose the appropriate size and shape of the implant. After a few minutes, both came out and the implant was finalized after a discussion with the doctors.

'What visuals did you show her in the side room?' I asked Jenny.

'I showed her a *Playboy*,' she replied.

'What is a *Playboy*?' I asked, pretending not to know.

'Come with me. I'll show you.'

In the counselling room, there were many issues of *Playboy* and *Penthouse* neatly arranged in racks. The assets of the topless models were being shown to the patients to help them point out the desired shape and size. I remembered that in our medical college hostel, the solitary, smuggled *Playboy* had been worth its weight in gold. It used to have an endless waiting list of borrowers.

This was a smart method, but would be difficult to implement in India. Even if there were no protests by moral brigades, sex-starved hospital employees would tear out the relevant pages and take them away.

The patient left the consultation room. It was time to recharge with a coffee break.

I brought up the subject again. 'Jenny, you showed me the magazine but did not tell me the meaning of the word 'playboy'.

'Ask Dr. Palmer. He has all the qualities of a playboy!'

'Thanks for enhancing my reputation!' said Dr. Palmer and laughed the loudest amongst the group.

Actually, Dr. Palmer was amongst the few people in the department who had been happily married for a long time. After getting to know that a majority of the staff had ill-fated marriages, I thought that the Indian arranged marriages were not so bad after all.

In the evening, I shifted to my apartment in the building next to the hospital. The next day, we were in the operation theatre.

There was pin drop silence in the waiting area. Most of the relatives were engrossed in books. It reminded me of the waiting area of our hospital in Delhi, which was way more interesting with all the animated chatter.

After entering the operation theatre complex, I found there was no vacant locker. Without hesitation, Dr. Palmer offered to share his with me.

The first patient on the operation list was a young lady undergoing liposuction.

'Good skin tone and localized fat excess make her an ideal candidate for liposuction,' Dr. Palmer said.

I scrutinized her carefully but could see just the slightest bulge. This was as fastidious as anybody could be about one's looks. I was reminded of my cousin Titu's wife Misha. She bugged Titu by calling him at his office whenever she was upset at gaining even two hundred grams.

I said, 'Chief, she seems to be fixated on microscopic flaws!'

'Rightly so. She is a supermodel. The few hundred grams of fat that we take out will be worth millions of dollars to her!' he said.

Dr. Palmer elucidated the nuances of each step of the operation that he carried out.

'Depending on the weight of the patient, we usually take out a maximum five to eight litres in one sitting. I have never had any serious problem with this amount.'

There was much clinical advice and many take home messages from him.

On the next operation day, the first patient was being put to sleep by Jeremy, the certified registered nurse anaesthetist. He was working under an anaesthesiologist doctor who was supervising the cases on a number of operation tables. The face lift operation was carried out and the next case was due in another fifteen minutes. I introduced myself to Jeremy. The *Golf Digest* magazine on his trolley caught my attention.

I asked him out of curiosity, 'Do you play golf?'

'Yes. In fact, that is what drives my life. What about you?'

He had probably expected to find a golfing buddy in me.

'Actually, there is no golf course near my home. So I was never introduced to the game,' I said and hastily exited the discussion.

I did not have the courage to tell him that the sport I had played the most was street cricket.

It was obvious that most hospital employees in America could aspire to a good lifestyle. On the contrary, the technicians in our hospitals were struggling to make ends meet.

Jeremy suggested I have a look at the adjacent operation theatre where another plastic surgeon, Dr. Martin was working. Dr. Martin graciously allowed me access to his operation theatre. There, I watched a familiar scene. Litres of the yellowish liquid fat were sucked out from the abdomen and thighs of a young lady and were being collected in transparent containers. But there was a twist. Some of the fat was purified and re-injected into the buttocks to make them perky like J. Lo's.

'I picked up the steps of this surgery from my visits to Brazil, the Mecca of plastic surgery. There, the main reason for the popularity of body shaping is the beach-oriented lifestyle. The commonest dating zone is not a restaurant but a beach. The formal dress code is a bikini for the girl and shorts for the boy!' Dr. Martin said.

I met Angela, a visiting plastic surgeon from Venezuela, in the same operation theatre. She was a classic Latin beauty with the figure of a *Sports Illustrated Swimsuit* model. After the surgeries were over, she invited me for a cup of coffee in the cafeteria.

'So, what do you know about Venezuela?' she asked.

'It is famous for two products, oil and Miss Universe! I must compliment you for maintaining yourself so well despite being a busy professional. You too could have been a beauty queen.'

My praise was spontaneous.

'Well, I started early.'

'Go on. Tell me all about your fitness mantras.'

'It has been a combination of workouts and plastic surgery. By the age of twenty, my sister and I had finished with the plastic surgeries we required. Our dad always cribs that it is very costly to bring up girls in Venezuela!'

'In India, fathers say the same, but at the time of the ostentatious marriage ceremony,' I said.

A week passed in a jiffy. The weekend was off for most of the staff, except those on emergency duty. On Friday evening, the question on everybody's lips was, 'What are you up to this weekend?'

Angela, the Venezuelan, asked me the same.

'I'll go canoeing and play golf.'

I could not conceal my grin while making the pretentious statement.

'A lot of Indians live in my neighbourhood. I know that you people do everything apart from these activities.'

'Okay, let us see what my sister and brother-in-law have in store for me. I will get back to you on Monday.'

I returned to Bhavya's house to a festive atmosphere in the evening. It was a big surprise to see legendary singer Surekha perform at their private party in the basement hall. Around twenty odd *desi* couples had been invited. Surekha regaled the gathering with her evergreen hits. Just before she left, I was introduced to her. I was lost for words but she acted like anyone else.

I roamed around the city and enjoyed the major attractions like the Sears Tower and the Adler Planetarium the next day. It was party time again in the evening. We went to a monthly gathering of families. To emphasize their desi heritage, the ladies were wearing heavily embroidered suits and sarees. I was surprised to find quite a few Pakistani couples. There was no barbed wire fence between the Indians and Pakistanis in Chicago. They were still going at each other's throats, but to embrace each other.

Most of the youngsters and kids had skipped the party. The gossip that generated the most excitement was about somebody's son or daughter fooling around with a Caucasian or an African-American.

On Sunday, I rang up Nandini.

'So, what have you learnt until now?'

'The best way to please a lady here is to gift her plastic surgery!'

'Better pay attention to the surgeries instead of the ladies. Strictly, no extension of your return air ticket.'

I was back to the hospital on Monday, which was the most hated day. Everyone was curious to find out what others did on the weekend, perhaps as a way to deal with their Monday blues.

That day, I was in the outpatient department. Upon entering the examination room, I noticed a young lady with a pinched nose. Any plastic surgeon worth his salt could tell that it had been a nose reshaping disaster. Excess of tissue had been removed. Dr. Palmer allowed her to speak.

'Doctor, I want my original nose back. There was only a mild broadening of the tip to begin with. But, because of the atrocious nose job by Dr. Gilbert, only aliens would ask me out on a date!'

'Don't worry. We will undo the damage and you will have plenty of suitors. But, I was wondering why you went to a doctor who is not a certified plastic surgeon,' Dr. Palmer asked.

'I was attracted by advertisements. Then, he cornered me with his smooth talking during the first consultation,' she revealed.

'See, there are such charlatans all across the globe. They bring a bad name to the whole fraternity of plastic surgeons,' Dr. Palmer said as he gestured to all the fellows.

We planned nasal reconstruction for her by using tissue from the ear cartilage.

As they say, similar cases often come in waves. Another lady called Aretha entered.

'Doctor, you operated on me a year ago to correct the hump on the bridge of my nose. The swelling has disappeared completely but I am still left with a small hump,' she said.

'The residual hump is not very significant. Since subjective judgment of the surgeon is involved in such surgeries, a mild problem may remain in some cases,' Dr. Palmer said.

Obviously, he was convincing her to accept her look.

'But I only had a mild problem to begin with!'

There was pin drop silence. Aretha had delivered the knockout punch to Dr. Palmer.

'Okay, we will do the revision surgery,' Dr. Palmer said to Aretha's delight.

After the patient had moved out of the chamber, Dr. Palmer addressed us. 'If you put a little bit of sugar in coffee, there is always scope to add more. But too much of it spoils the whole cup. So, it is always better to undercorrect because overcorrection is more difficult to manage. Minor revisions and touch-ups are a part and parcel of plastic surgery. That is why you should be friends with the patient and vice versa!'

From the next operation day, I was asked to scrub in on the procedures. It made me feel more involved. During that week, we did a variety of procedures, some of which were opposite to each other. On a Wednesday morning, we performed a lip reduction for a protruding lower lip. However, in the afternoon, a patient had a lip augmentation by fat injection.

On Friday, there was a buzz that a celebrity would be visiting. I went to Rick, the receptionist who confirmed that Dorothy Williams, the star comedian, had an appointment. We doubted whether Dr. Palmer would allow his fellows to be present while he was examining her.

Dorothy was the first on the morning appointment list. As she entered, Dr. Palmer gestured for us to move out.

'Please, let them stay. I like to have a lot of people around me,' Dorothy said.

We were happy to be allowed in. Dorothy looked to be in her early fifties. Her eyebrows were artificially high but the lower part of her face had begun sagging.

'What changes do you want to your face?' Dr. Palmer asked.

'I am a celebrity because of my umpteen plastic surgeries. It makes me happy when other comedians earn their living making fun of me. So, operate on me in such a way that I remain a living cartoon!'

'Dorothy, you spread cheer wherever you go,' Dr. Palmer said.

The weekend was going to be special yet again. On Saturday evening, Bhavya, Manik and I set out for the astronomy meet. From the main freeway to Wisconsin, we turned into a country road. Soon, we came across the banners of the Illinois Star Gazers Club. We walked to a small valley which had no artificial light.

The view of the sky was unlike any other I had seen before. Even the satellites were visible as moving, star-like objects. The astronomy aficionados had brought huge telescopes which were mounted on their trucks. They enthusiastically showed us planets, star clusters, galaxies, and nebulae through them. We left the venue only at dawn, after cursing the sun for ending the grand spectacle!

Life was on a roll, high on fun and learning, but without any responsibility. Of course, that was too good to last. As I began fitting into the hospital system, the departure date also started approaching. During the last week of my stay, I decided to take off from the hospital. A departmental farewell party was organized for me and another fellow. There was an exchange of visiting cards and promises to keep in touch.

Dr. Palmer was in a reflective mood. 'I am a Western Anglo-Saxon Protestant. Yet, I identify myself with plastic surgeons, even though they may be from different cultures. We treasure the ecstatic smile of a lady who sees her corrected face for the first time after surgery. But, on some bad days, there might be a call in the evening, for a patient who developed haematoma after surgery. Still, in my next birth also, I would like to be a plastic surgeon. We are the ones who can bring the average lookers on par with those who have been gifted good looks by god.'

With a heavy heart, I bade farewell to the plastic surgery team at the Lakeview Hospital. On reaching Bhavya's house, I contacted my old pal Parveen. He lived in a small town in the state of Kansas. Parveen sounded very happy to hear from me. I requested him to come over.

'I will push off tomorrow morning, and reach in about eight hours.'

'Do bring your wife and kid along, too.'

'*Saley*! I am coming alone because I want to shower you with lots of abuses.'

So, the guy who used to fight with me over the hostel washroom was now driving four hundred miles, just to meet me.

He was at my doorstep by the next afternoon.

'Rascal, you did not find time to contact me for the last two years! What do you think of yourself!' he shouted when he saw me.

'Relax, Parveen. The pressure of plastic surgery residency forced me into a shell. Old friendships do not end over such trivial matters.'

We went to the basement bar and remembered our college days. The conversation ultimately shifted to the subject of Manika.

'Did you contact her?' Parveen asked.

I made up an explanation about her.

'No, I thought I would call her up once before I left.'

'So, you've kept her on the accessory list? The way she talks about you, I can make out her feelings for you.'

I thought about Manika. She had not tried to contact me since our last meeting, even though she had seemed to be keen on doing so. She was probably unsure of my feelings for her.

'Parveen, it's too late. Both of us have travelled too far on separate paths. She opted to leave me herself.'

I was acting tough. But, I had a resurgence of affection for her.

I called Manika the day before my return flight.

'Why didn't you call me earlier? You could have visited me in Los Angeles. But it's not too late. Just postpone your ticket for now,' she said excitedly.

'It's not possible at this stage. My schedule was too tight to make it to Los Angeles. On my next visit here, I will plan to meet you in advance.'

Her voice grew sadder. She understood I had avoided getting in touch with her. We talked for a few more minutes, but there was no spark in our conversation.

The Reluctant Migrant

A day before my departure from America, a call from Nandini made me go ballistic. She was arriving at Delhi Airport to receive me. Nandini had coordinated her leave with my return, just to make me feel special.

After my arrival, I hardly suffered jet lag as I spent the next twenty-four hours in Nandini's arms, in a dark room! We mused a lot over the blossoming of our romance.

'Do you know that before we even started talking to each other, I could tell you were captivated by me?' Nandini said.

'How? Was it the way I looked at you? But a gorgeous girl like you would get looks from a lot of guys anyway.'

'That was just one of the clues. There were many other giveaways. After seeing me, your right hand would slip into your trouser pocket and your face turned red.'

'Stop it! Do not expose me completely! Your powers of observation are amazing.'

In the evening, we entered a greeting card shop in the South Extension market. As we were browsing through the cards, a stunning lady entered the shop. My gaze involuntarily followed her.

'Hey, what is going on? Your roving eye is active even in my presence. After I leave, your lechery might cross all limits,' Nandini said.

She seemed to have an extra wide field of vision.

'Nandini, be a sport. I keep studying faces to develop my aesthetic sense!' I grinned.

Anyway, she had caught me on the wrong foot.

We talked about my future plans at a Thai restaurant that evening. After all, I was technically an educated and unemployed youth.

'Logically, I should settle in Delhi. What do you think?'

'I will follow you like a good wife. But do consider a cosy nest in Assam.'

'Once you get used to life in a metro, it's difficult to adjust to the slow lanes in the small towns. I do think about settling in a tea garden, but after retirement. But that will always remain a fantasy because practically, doctors rarely move cities once they have an established practice. Their patients also do not want to let go of a trusted doctor.'

Nandini left two days later. As her train slowly chugged out of sight, I felt forlorn.

In the evening, Mom, Dad and I were enjoying a conversation after a long time. Dad looked imposing with his big moustache. My mom referred to the upturned ends as the hands of a clock at ten minutes past ten! Dad classified people into just two categories, Peshawaris and non-Peshawaris, and in his typical Pathan salwar kurta, he seemed to have come straight from his ancestral town Peshawar.

'As long as Nandini was around, Dhruv never looked elsewhere!' Dad said to Mom.

'It seems like you have forgotten the time we were newly married. You used to hold my hand constantly as if I was going to fly away,' Mom said with a dreamy look.

Then, she turned to me, 'What is next? We have very little insight into your profession. So, you have to work out the future by yourselves.'

'I have got a job offer from the Rainbow Hospital in Saket, which is so close to our home. This means that your son and hopefully daughter-in-law will keep you company. You can forget about a peaceful life!'

I expected my parents to be delighted at the prospect of me putting up with them in their twilight years.

'Why don't you go to Mumbai and become a plastic surgeon for film stars and models?' Dad asked.

His bombastic suggestion made me uneasy, as it could have been an early sign of dementia or a psychiatric problem.

'Dad, are you feeling okay? Let me massage your head with mustard oil,' I said.

'I'm all right. But, your enthusiasm seems to have died!' Dad replied.

'Dad, it is not easy to settle in an expensive city like Mumbai. Additionally, there are quite a few well-established plastic surgeons there.'

'Come on, Dhruv! You belong to a clan that has given so many actors and directors to the Hindi film industry. These people made it big by venturing out of their comfort zone and boarding the Frontier Mail. However, you will not have to struggle much because I will support you financially.'

Dad was very resolute. I was stimulated by his words but could not digest the prospect of slogging for many more years to come. Only someone setting up a winery could be that patient.

If I settled in Delhi, my circle of friends and relatives was sure to give an impetus to my career. I even promised to work on their faces and bodies so they were in a class beyond compare!

In the morning, Dad left for some work. Mom and I were relaxing in the veranda.

'Mom, why does Dad want to push me away? There is no dearth of opportunities in this town,' I said.

'Beta, your dad has always given you a lot of independence. Even now, he has merely suggested, not ordered anything. There was a missed opportunity in your dad's life and he wants to make amends for it.'

'Oh! It seems that there are some family secrets that have been kept from me? Come on, Mom, tell me everything,' I said.

'You know very well that your dad survives on Hindi movies. In his youth, he was damn handsome and also used to take part in the local theatre. He had a serious wish to be on the big screen. Since he was the eldest in a joint family, he had a lot of responsibilities. So, he could not muster the courage to leave his family as well as his job. Even after our marriage, he had dreams about Bollywood. I feared that I would meet the same fate as some of the first wives of the stars! So, I coaxed him into leading a householder's life.'

'But, why was I kept in the dark?'

'Rajinder is so touchy about this topic that I avoid discussing it altogether. Some of our relatives, who shifted to Bombay around that time, established themselves in the film industry. He felt left out. To come to terms with his shattered dreams, he acquired the look of a typical bureaucrat. But now, he would like to rectify some of his mistakes through you.'

'But why are you supporting him in this?'

'Nobody knows you better than your mother. You have tremendous potential and I want you to realize it. I don't want to use my children as crutches for old age.'

'Thank you, Mom!'

I went to Dr. Vidur, for his take on the situation.

'A calculated risk is often required to get ahead in life. Being equipped with a superspecialist degree, you have an edge. I can recommend you to a few plastic surgeons in Mumbai. In the worst case scenario, you can always return to Delhi and join me,' he said.

It seemed like my dad and the others enjoyed watching me battle the odds. However, the Frontier Mail was the trigger that fired my imagination.

For two days, I pondered over the decision, but the see-saw kept moving. Finally, my dad's poignant tale tilted it in favour of the tinsel town. I decided I would go by the Frontier Mail instead of the Rajdhani Express, so as to be a toiler right from day one.

But I suddenly realized that I had finalized my future without having so much as a word with the person who would be most affected. I dialled Nandini's number immediately.

'Close your eyes! I have a surprise for you,' I said.

'I am about to make a child cry by putting in an intravenous line. Talk to me fast.'

'We are now going to be living life on the fast lane in Bollywood!'

'People sober up after marriage, but your ideas get weirder. I'm sure that your uncles must have pushed you into this venture.'

'What difference does a city make? I will still return home to your arms every evening.'

'So, what is your game plan?'

'Maverick's plan in reverse. I have visualized my destination but have to chart out the course.'

'I will not be able to join you for a couple of years. But my good wishes will always be with you.'

I rang up a few of my old friends in Mumbai the next morning. Dr. Alok Shah came up with a workable idea.

'Practicing in Mumbai straightaway would be like jumping into the water without knowing how to swim. I think it will be better if you initially do a job to get the feel of the city and then plan further.'

'I understand what you mean but most of the jobs in hospitals involve less cosmetic surgery and more trauma and reconstructive surgery.'

'I will discuss this issue with a few local doctors and get back to you soon.'

I got a call from him the same evening.

'I think you should approach Dr. Vijay Jayaraj. He performs cosmetic surgeries on celebrities. Due to the heavy workload, he usually has one plastic surgeon as an associate. Right now there is a vacancy.'

'But, do I stand a chance?'

'Definitely. He prefers outsiders as they usually return to their own town after a year or so. Local plastic surgeons could become competitors in his backyard after learning the tricks of the trade.'

'But what if he asks me about my future plans?'

'Tell him you plan to move back to Delhi after gaining some experience because your old parents need support.'

'You mean I should lie to him?'

'Shri Raja Harish Chandra ji, please leave your honesty for some other time! One does not commit a heinous crime by lying about a few facts.'

'Okay, I get your point.'

To initiate contact with Dr. Jayaraj, I requested Dr. Vidur to have a word with him.

After a few hours, I got a call from Dr. Vidur.

'I have recommended you to Dr. Jayaraj. He has asked me to send you for an interview.'

'Thank you so much, sir.'

'Apart from my persuasion, the reputation of our department has helped you. So, do uphold the prestige of your parent institute. I had to tell Dr. Jayaraj a lot of lies about your capabilities. I called you a very dynamic person but did not reveal that you alternate between being slightly foolish and very foolish!'

I knew that the chief was just being sarcastic. He had been proclaiming to everyone that I was one of his best students.

Next day, I fixed an appointment with Dr. Jayaraj. There was just about a week's time to prepare for the interview. I booked my ticket in the Frontier Mail, renamed the Golden Temple Mail. During the week, I studied frenetically.

I boarded the train at the Hazrat Nizamuddin station and got a window seat. There wasn't any time for a *Bharat darshan* through the window! I used the time to brush up on my subject. As I alighted at the platform, I stomped my feet and clenched my fists.

Dr. Jayaraj called me to his office. He was dressed impeccably and clean shaven. Like many overachievers, he was fidgety.

I was asked about the recent advances in the subject. But, he did not enquire about my future plans, perhaps on the presumption that the *Punju* boy could not miss the butter chicken belt for long! The appointment letter was immediately handed to me.

So, I became a part of the Tulip Plastic Surgery Centre at Versova. The flat allotted to me was just two kilometres away from the hospital. So, I was likely to escape the traffic. Since the flat was on the eleventh floor, the cool sea breeze entered it freely.

A celebrity visited the hospital on my first day itself. The lanky lass, Momi, entered through a back door to the secret waiting area. The stars were obviously segregated from the commoners. I was told that some of the stars opted to be operated on at odd hours. It was a different kind of underworld, and the only weapon that was allowed was the surgeon's knife!

'You will come across a lot of celebrities in my clinic. It is our utmost duty to protect their secrecy as they have shown faith in us. When you meet people outside the hospital, avoid giving away the identity of our clients,' Dr. Jayaraj said to me that day.

After a few days, I noticed that Dr. Jayaraj was a stickler for check-lists. He had one made for almost every task and ensured they were displayed all over the hospital. I wondered if he had them in his home as well, including one for making love.

There was a poster with the words 'Do not discuss clients' even in the hospital lift.

One week later, in the operation theatre, the technicians and nursing staff were huddled in a corner. They were talking in hushed tones. Amongst them was the head technician, Murari, a man with an unassuming appearance.

'Murari ji, am I in too?' I asked.

'Doctor sahib, the first case on the list is the film star Saajan. He will be undergoing a revision face lift,' he said in a hushed voice.

'Where did he get his first face lift?' I asked Murari.

'Fifteen years back, in the US. At that time, plastic surgery facilities here were not so advanced. But now, he cannot even afford to get operated abroad. Someone told me that he had to switch to local brands of whisky from premium Scotch!'

'Dr. Jayaraj has told me to keep mum about all the celebrities who get operated here,' I said.

'Sometimes reporters from film magazines try to extract information from the staff, but we have never obliged them. We gossip, but just amongst ourselves. The fascinating job provides us the kick we need in life. So, offers with better pay are given a miss.'

As Murari and I were about to share the next scandalous tidbit, Saajan entered the operation theatre. Even wrinkles could not diminish his aura. The incorrigible romantic waved to everyone. The hearts of the women staff must have skipped a beat or two.

Pointing towards Dr. Jayaraj, he said, 'You doctors are hardcore communists. You make the kings and paupers wear the same clothes!'

'Why not? Every human has the same organs and tissues on the inside,' Dr. Jayaraj commented.

'You are wrong in one aspect. Instead of blood, tomato ketchup will ooze from my body!' Saajan grinned.

Then he faced the staff and said, 'I have always escaped unscathed from villains, knives, but Jayaraj's sharp scalpel will get the better of me.'

'But even a wink from the heroine made you collapse on the ground!' Murari chimed in.

Everyone in the operation theatre laughed heartily but Dr. Jayaraj and I were the picture of unease. A revision facelift was more treacherous and tedious compared to when you did it the first time.

As the operation began, my hands started to tremble, but I soon steadied them. Due to the previous surgery, there were multiple adhesions. Even one wrong nick of the scissors could injure the branches of the facial nerve. A delicate balance of caution and bravado helped us make steady progress.

Despite effective air-conditioning, beads of perspiration were visible on Dr. Jayaraj's forehead. They were threatening to coalesce and fall onto the operative field. One person was required just to wipe them off repeatedly with gauze.

As soon as Saajan regained consciousness after the surgery, we checked his facial movements for signs of nerve injury. Thankfully, everything was okay.

Saajan stayed in the hospital for two days. But he made a lot of new fans because of his unique ability to laugh at himself. On the day he was being discharged, I changed his dressing and gave him all the necessary instructions.

'I hope that you will be able to get better roles after the facelift,' I said to him.

'I will still be playing a father or uncle in most movies. But for this surgery, the only role available to me would have been the *Betaal* holding up prince Vikram!'

Just two days after Saajan's discharge, there was a buzz that a pretty actress, Rosina, was going to be admitted for nose reshaping. But, right from the time she entered the hospital, it was clear that she was a freak rose with oversized thorns that reached the petals. Just one hit had made her believe she was God's gift. At the time of admission, she found the private room, with all its worldly comforts, not up to her snooty standards.

'A person accustomed to staying in seven star hotels is being put up in a shabby lodge! If it were not for my faith in

Dr. Jayaraj, I would have moved out by now,' she told Sister Mary, the nurse in-charge.

Mary was shell-shocked because even Dr. Jayaraj had never talked to her in a contemptuous tone.

Even on the rare occasions that Rosina was polite, she harped on about her forthcoming movie. Fed up of her *main main*, we nicknamed her '*Bakri* 'and vowed never to watch her movies! All of us fervently prayed she would leave the hospital as soon as possible.

Two days after Rosina's surgery, Mary and I barged into Dr. Jayaraj's office. Sensing we were on the warpath, Dr. Jayaraj told us to sit down and ordered coffee.

'Does this have something to do with Rosina's behaviour?'

'You guessed it, sir. She addresses me as "hey nurse." Please depute somebody else to look after her,' Mary fumed.

I added, 'Today, I went to her room to change her dressing. First, she kept chatting on the mobile for five minutes. Then, she refused to let me do the dressing and said she hadn't paid such a hefty fee to get followed up by a greenhorn. Kindly go to her room and do the needful.'

'Relax. Take this as an opportunity to learn how to deal with snobs. I appreciate both of you for acting with the utmost restraint despite repeated provocation. Actually, the quick rise in her film career has gone to her head. If she puts on airs everywhere, new projects will start drying up because it is only the superstars who can get away with tantrums. Anyway, I will discharge her after the rounds. Then, we will have a departmental party.'

Dr. Jayaraj was surely an expert in the art of pacifying.

On his way to Rosina's room, he insisted that I come along.

'I don't want to ruin my day,' I said.

'Trust me. She will not dare to act smart in my presence.'

To my surprise, he cornered Rosina on entering the room. 'Why did you refuse a dressing by Dr. Dhruv?'

Rosina was taken aback. She was at a loss for words.

Dr. Jayaraj continued, 'If I have sent him to do your dressing, it means I have full faith in him. In fact, if I was to have a plastic surgery myself, I would want to be operated on by Dr. Dhruv since I am passing on all my skills to him.'

'Actually, since I was a child, I have been extremely afraid of hospitals and doctors. That's the reason I've been overreacting to every situation in the hospital.'

So, a much mellower Rosina was on the defensive even though her over-sized ego prevented her from apologizing.

We left the private room.

'Sir, I really appreciate the stand you took at the cost of losing your client,' I said to Dr. Jayaraj.

'To tell you the truth, I have reached a stage where I am the one in demand. Initially, I used to chase the patients, but now, they chase me! But as is emphasized in some ads, these actions are performed by experts. Do not try them at home!

Starstruck

On a leisurely day at the end of the month, Dr. Jayaraj called me into his office for a cup of tea.

'Sir, you are amongst the pioneers of plastic surgery in India. The first few years must have been very demanding.'

'Everyone envies me for my roaring practice. But the initial phase was like devising a new route through a jungle. In the seventies, there was no place in India where one could be properly trained in cosmetic surgery. One needed to go abroad to pick up the techniques. So, I had to beg foreign surgeons at various conferences to accept me as a fellow. I was even called a leech by my colleagues! But they had to eat their words later on.'

'How did you make your way into showbiz?'

'I started my practice during the early eighties. In keeping with the times, the leading ladies started wearing revealing dresses. As their necklines started to plunge, the number of surgeries on my operation list began to increase! Not to be left behind, even the heroes started going shirtless. The fashion and modelling industry also started gaining ground. As plastic surgeons, we had to modify the techniques learnt abroad to suit Indian patients.'

'True. The Indian race is unique. We have bony facial features resembling Caucasians and overlying skin nearer to the Africans,' I added.

'Yes. The thicker skin is advantageous in nose reshaping as minor imperfections do not show. On the other hand our scars are more prominent as compared to the Caucasians.'

He continued, 'Doctors can make a big difference in people's lives with small gestures. This is precisely why I have called you here. I want you to accompany us for the free surgical camp. Tomorrow, we are leaving for a rural area in the Beed district of Maharashtra where we will operate on people who have deformities due to birth defects, burns and injuries.'

'How did you start this NGO?' I asked.

'A few years back, my cosmetic surgery practice began to boom. So, there wasn't any time for other types of plastic surgery. I started seeing myself as a self serving doctor. Then, a friend invited me to Lions Club as a guest. They roped me as a member of the service organization and I decided to chip in with my contribution. With the help of two other doctors, I organize these camps every three months.'

'I would love to accompany you,' I said.

The next day, we left our bustling metro for the countryside. In the last hour of the journey, the resilience of our backs was thoroughly tested by the bumpy road. However, our jolly driver was unfazed. According to him, the road had been deliberately left in that condition to prevent drivers from dozing off! At last, we reached the campsite at a local charitable hospital.

For the next three days, our charged-up team worked late into the night, correcting birth-defects and deformities. We did not want to disappoint the patients, some of whom had travelled a considerable distance.

After receiving the first pay cheque, I dumped the pager and upgraded to a mobile phone. However, I gave my number to only a few people so as to avoid the costly incoming calls. Just three days after my proud acquisition, the mobile rang for the first time. I almost pressed the red button in my excitement.

'Hi, Dr. Dhruv? This is Nirdosh Khanna.'

My right hand began to shake. I couldn't believe the legendary villain Nirdosh Khanna was talking to me. Though he was a relative, he had never visited us in Delhi.

'Your dad has requested me to contact you. Let us meet for dinner on Saturday at my house.'

'Oh! It would be an honour.'

'So, mark the date. Remember the consequences of ignoring Rakka, the don,' he added in a melodramatic voice.

I reached his sea-facing apartment in Juhu on Saturday evening. Security had been briefed and I had a smooth passage.

'Do not be fooled by his image. He is very caring. The only time he cheats is when he steals sweets from the refrigerator!' his charming wife, Sandhya, said.

'I had to wait seven long years to get my first big break. However, a few months later, the same producers who snubbed me were queuing up to see me. So, I can relate to the strugglers. Your father's contribution to his extended family cannot be repaid. He even deferred his marriage for a few years so the younger ones could stand on their own feet. I was able to move to this city because of his promise to look after my parents. When you were an infant, you often used to play in my lap and once even wetted my clothes!' Nirdosh said.

'Some of your fans are upset as in recent years you have taken the role of an honourable man. Are you trying to change your image?' I asked.

'The trend of heroes taking a negative role brought about a crisis for villains. To survive, we had to take up character and comedy roles. The industry is ruthless. Losers have no place here,' he reflected.

'What do you think is the scope for plastic surgery in this city?'

'Well, it is going to be big in the future. If you show good results, I will definitely recommend you to my friends,' he said.

Sandhya intervened, 'Doctor, do I require any procedure? Sorry for bringing up something which should be discussed in your clinic but I cannot resist taking advantage of a plastic surgeon's presence in my home.'

'You are not the only one obsessed with looks. Once I went to a party in Delhi. A distant relative of mine got to know I was doing a plastic surgery course. She got so carried away, she lifted her dress there and then to show me her sagging lower abdomen. But now, even men are becoming more conscious about how they look.'

I scanned Sandhya's face for any imperfections. She had chiselled features with well-defined cheek bones. There were no wrinkles, open pores or blemishes.

'Your face does not require any alteration. In fact, I could use you as a reference when I am planning for other ladies,' I said.

'Thanks. I feel good. After all, a professional view is the most accurate.'

After my skilful compliments, she looked as blissful as the Mona Lisa!

Nirdosh interrupted. He shifted to his filmy voice.

'Doctor, you seem to be enamoured with her. Flirting with Rakka's wife means inviting third degree torture!'

'Boss, I lose both ways. If I found any fault, I would still have been punished!'

'Smart boy. If you can tackle Rakka, you will be able to deal with all the eccentrics of Bollywood.'

'Nirdosh, stop the acting and take his advice about your face and body,' Sandhya said.

'There are so many things wrong with me, it would require scores of procedures to get them fixed. But I am aware that I will never be cast as a hero. So it is better to stick with my devilish look.

On my way back, I was escorted right up to the gate by the couple.

'Never feel alone in this city. You are always welcome here,' Nirdosh said.

On the way back to my house, I thought of my dad. Nirdosh had showered me with so much affection only because of him. I realized that, like a goalkeeper, my mind had been pre-occupied with anticipating unpleasant surprises. So an unexpected invitation from a bigwig was all the more satisfying.

When Nandini called me up the next day, it felt like a bonus. 'I will be reaching Mumbai in a month.'

'I look forward to walking in the rain with you, just like in those old movies.'

During the entire week, Dr. Jayaraj was mostly on leave. Even when he was around, he seemed to be in his own world. I did not have the courage to ask him directly. So I called on Murari, the nosiest person in the department.

'Murari ji, Dr. Jayaraj seems to have abandoned this hospital. What is the matter?'

'Doctor sahib, there has to be a solid reason. He has rarely been on leave. Even with a fever or a stomach ache, he would carry on with his work. Once, he told me that when he was a junior doctor, his bosses would forcibly send him on leave for a few days every year.'

'Has he hooked up with one of the classy ladies? Old people are known to get extremely infatuated.'

'That is highly improbable. His attachment to his wife could put a newly married couple to shame! He still calls her every few hours,' Murari replied.

The following Monday, Dr. Jayaraj called on me.

'Dhruv, you must be wondering whether I have gone bonkers. I wanted to speak my mind but I was in a dilemma.'

'What happened, sir?'

'It was a tough decision. But, I have finalized my plans to relocate to Dubai.'

'What!' I felt the earth move beneath my feet.

'It might seem like I am being too recklessly adventurous at this age.'

'Exactly. Most of the young plastic surgeons, including me, aspire to be in your position.'

'Sometimes it gets very lonely at the top. I've had a lot of professional acclaim and have made a lot of money. I need new goals to reclaim my zest for life.'

'You would have to build your practice from scratch there, brick by brick.'

'Some of my friends also have similar reservations. Our society is deeply biased against old people. When the young make bold career moves, they are said to be go-getters. But an old risk taker is labelled demented. Actually, my situation is unique. The idea of setting up a clinic in Dubai was suggested by my celebrity clients. They want total anonymity while getting their treatment. Despite our best efforts, it is not possible to keep everything under wraps here in Mumbai. Above all, the main reason for re-locating there is my son; he is settled there. I yearn to play with my grandchildren.'

'I heard that you get paid very well there.'

'That is true. So, I just need to do one-fourth of the work that I do here. You must be aware that many eminent plastic surgeons from USA, Europe and Brazil have set up practices in the Gulf region.'

'What about the local Arab populace? Do they go under the knife?'

'Yes, in a big way. The society may look conservative. However, the young Arabs are quite finicky about their looks. One of my friends is practicing plastic surgery in Dubai. He told me that if he does a good job, many ladies bring him flowers.'

'Chief, please reconsider your decision. This place survives on your name.'

'I know that there's bound to be insecurity among the staff. How can I let down people like Murari and Mary who have supported me for so long. I want this place to remain as busy as it is now. That is the reason I want you to take charge,' he said.

The finger that he pointed at me felt like a revolver.

'Me? How will I sustain this whole setup? Hardly anybody in town knows me.'

I was still stupefied.

'As a tried and tested fellow, you get the first offer. I don't want the wrong person getting entrenched here. Your ambition will provide you with the strength to overcome the expected initial hiccups. It is obviously your choice if you want to accept the offer. Remember that such opportunities come once in a while. I propose to give you the entire set up on rent basis. So, there won't be any day to day interference in your work.

However, I will be there for you...like a twenty-four hour helpline. And you have just one day to decide.'

'Thanks for trusting me. I will carefully weigh all the pros and cons because this will be my own decision. So, I will not be able to blame my parents if things go wrong!' I replied.

By the time I reached home, I ran into a mental roadblock. By refusing the offer, I would miss the boat altogether.

The encouragement from my near and dear ones shut off the negatives in my mind and I conveyed my acceptance the next day.

Dr. Jayaraj left two weeks later. During that period, he did not discuss academics with me. Rather, he tried to imbue me with the nitty-gritty of running a plastic surgery set up. Dr. Jayaraj listed the employees who were motivated by appreciation, those who required periodic rough treatment as well as those who required doses of both.

The Struggler

There was no choice for the abandoned young bird but to take the flight. It was my first day as chief. I realized that all these years I had been foolish to find faults with bosses who had actually been protecting me. That day, I had to tackle medical as well as administrative issues on my own. And I was no expert in talking my way out of all situations.

'Is there a motive behind Dr. Jayaraj's generosity? He could probably not find any takers for the hospital at such short notice. So he dumped it on me by disguising it as a great favour,' I said to myself.

Then the phone rang. As expected, it was Nandini.

'My best wishes for your first day. I feel awful. Should have been there to see you off with a lipstick mark on your cheek! I am missing out on so many golden moments of our life because of this stupid post graduation,' she said.

'Without doing an M.D., a career-minded girl like you would have become a whining machine! So, enjoy your academic confinement for some more time. But I promise we will have a great time when you get here next month.'

During my first day at the office, I tried to interact with as many employees as possible. That unearthed many hidden stories about the hospital! The longest exchange was with Murari, whose never say die attitude could be of immense help in odd situations.

He told me, 'The surgeon gets all the credit but technicians and nurses do so many critical tasks behind the scenes. When Dr. Jayaraj was in a tight corner during surgeries, my suggestions would often save the day. In fact, whenever I went on leave, Dr. Jayaraj postponed complicated surgeries till I joined again.

'I do agree that the surgeon gets more recognition. However, he also receives the badge of infamy. Once you come out of the hospital building, you can hit a milk bar or a beer bar and then sleep in peace. But the surgeon passes a sleepless night in case of any complication because he is the visible face of the surgical team.'

Three uneventful days passed. On Thursday, soon after I had started examining the outpatients, the receptionist Divya rushed into my office.

'Sir, a man wants to get his fingerprints changed. Should I make his file?'

I looked at the CCTV that showed the reception. Divya pointed to a villainous looking man with a heavy moustache.

'Tell him that Dr. Dhruv is in a meeting and will be free after fifteen minutes.'

Before I could think any further, I received a call from the local don Shrikant.

He said, 'Doctor, I know a person named Vilas. He will be visiting you. Kindly do whatever is possible for him.'

Shrikant was soft spoken, but if he was opposed, his maliciousness often dragged on like generational family feuds. I was at my wits' end. So, I decided to use my preferred lifeline – phone the boss.

Luckily, I connected to Dr. Vidur immediately.

'Do not even touch the case. Technically, it is possible to change fingerprints. But, you would be party to any crime or fraud committed by the patient,' Dr. Vidur said.

It was obvious that I had to avoid operating on the thug at any cost. But a blunt refusal would have meant angering the don. I called for Murari and told him about the situation. He seemed to be even more confused than me. But after a few moments, his face brightened as if a deity had spoken to him.

'Doctor ji, you leave it to me,' he said and went to the waiting hall.

I watched the scene on the CCTV from my office. Murari sat by Vilas' side. They talked with each other for about two minutes. Then, Vilas got up and rushed out of the building. Murari came back to my office with a triumphant smile.

'Mission accomplished. That man will not bother us again.'

'But how did you do it so fast?'

'After becoming familiar with him, I made him come out with his intentions. Then, I whispered to him that the police commissioner of Mumbai had sent a circular to all plastic surgery clinics to report about any person coming to get their fingerprints changed. I offered to let him get away without registration. He pushed off immediately after thanking me profusely.'

Both of us had a hearty laugh at the macho man's vanishing act.

That night, Ajit, my favourite villain, appeared in my dream. I did Mona's plastic surgery while the 'smart boy Robert' and 'the lion' prodded me with revolvers.

The next day, I examined a simpleton named Baburao, who had a big scar on his face due to a previous accident. He wanted it to be erased completely.

Telling him the technical details would have been akin to explaining the theory of relativity to a Haryanvi wrestler.

I purposely kept it short and simple. 'There will be a lot of improvement with plastic surgery. However, the mark will not go away fully. Like diamonds, scars are forever. Even the world's wealthiest people cannot get rid of them completely.'

'But I work a lot in the sun. The plastic might melt!' he said.

I suppressed my laughter with great difficulty and explained, 'Plastic is not required in most plastic surgeries, including the one planned for you. Sometimes, plastic like materials are put in as implants.'

'Okay, do whatever you want, but make it better.'

After Baburao had left, a boy in his late teens entered my office with his parents. He had a nose with a grossly bulbous tip which seemed to be crying out for correction.

'Doctor, please help me. Since I was a young child, my classmates and friends have been giving me all sorts of nicknames. Now, in college, the girls have started calling me "the endangered species of Kaziranga". I cannot take it anymore.'

His father intervened, 'The younger generation is willing to go to ridiculous lengths for their appearance. As a yoga teacher, I feel that it is the inner self which needs to be polished.'

He seemed to have come reluctantly after bowing down to the majority in the family. After a while, the man left to get reports. His wife could not control herself any further.

She said, "Mr high character" is always ready with his sermons. He may forget his *pranayama,* but has never missed any movie starring Aisha. Whenever he watches the serial Kkamini, he does *dhyana yoga,* focused on Kavita Somani! Doctor, just ignore him and go ahead with the surgery.'

The whole team bent over backwards to get the hospital viable and running. I personally attended to every emergency, even if my sweet dreams were rudely shattered! Still, within a fortnight, our inflow of plastic surgery cases declined dramatically. The showbiz crowd was bypassing us. However, I was optimistic that we would get back on track soon.

Sunday was an exceptionally hot day, even by Mumbai's standards. I wished for more pleasant weather. Nandini was coming by flight even though she had to shell out her salary of two months. The ridiculously long train journey would have cut her holiday in half. While waiting outside the arrival terminal, I spotted her near the luggage belt. She stood out, even in the hep airport crowd and that made me feel really blessed.

When she arrived at the apartment, her eyes brightened. It was our first proper home. I took her to the balcony to let her have the feel of Mumbai's urban landscape.

A gust of westerly wind swept against us. Thick, dark clouds from the Arabian Sea were moving inland quickly. Soon, heavy rain started and we had to move indoor.

'The breakout of the monsoon has coincided with your homecoming,' I said excitedly.

The same evening, I told Nirdosh Khanna that Nandini was keen on meeting him.

'Come on over to Sunshine Hotel on Saturday. I'm having a bash for my friends. You will get to see the stars unplugged,' Nirdosh said.

Nandini was not heavily into Bollywood movies but watched most of the big hits.

'You must be looking forward to mixing with the actors at Nirdosh's party,' I said to Nandini.

'To be frank, although I do enjoy Hindi movies, I do not have a very high opinion about Bollywood as a whole. They just reinforce certain stereotypes.'

'What do you mean?

'Most of the successful heroes in Hindi cinema have been either Punjabis or Khans. This conveys that only a few ethnic groups represent the ideal Indian male. Tell me, how many people from the Northeast have made it big in Bollywood movies?'

Nandini and I had never had any serious political discussion before.

'But you have chosen a North Indian for yourself,' I said.

After realizing that she had made me uncomfortable, Nandini hugged me.

'Darling, do not get me wrong. The grouse against typecasting of characters in Hindi movies is shared by so many people across the country.'

On Saturday evening, we were all set for Nirdosh's party. In a matter of an hour, Nandini changed her look from a child specialist to a party specialist. But I dressed as if I was going to work. When we reached the Sunshine Hotel, I noticed the hotel staff staring at me. They seemed to be puzzled at my genre because of my plain clothes.

To make me feel at home, Nirdosh personally introduced me to the guests.

'He is the wizard of plastic surgery. I can vouch for his expertise.'

I never expected him to project me in such a way. I ended up being the centre of attention as everyone was curious to know about the latest updates on plastic surgery. But no one made any direct queries, which was understandable. Stars usually projected themselves as rare mutants with the absence of an ageing gene! However, I made an effort to entice them by being extra nice.

The party was livened up by the presence of Chitra, the gossip columnist of the hottest selling movie magazine, *Starsworld*. She had achieved stardom at a young age, in her own way. We enjoyed her company the most as she made even complete strangers feel comfortable around her.

She took Nandini and me to a corner and said, 'You might be under the impression that all these stars hate me. We do have occasional tiffs, especially when I reveal the naked truth about them. But actually, I am friends with most of them. They plot many scandals themselves to grab eyeballs. People are more interested in reading about who is sleeping with whom in a film magazine rather than scholarly articles!'

'So, you must be having a good time at these parties.'

'I do. I poke the stars and enjoy myself! But Nirdosh is a darling. He is one of the few people in the industry with a heart of gold.'

'What do you think about plastic surgery?' I asked Chitra.

'I think about it every day. When I come to these parties, I stick out like a sore thumb due to my average looks. So, I have a deep desire to change myself completely. I have met a few plastic surgeons. But, it has been said that it would be almost impossible for me to look like a model. What do you think?'

I scrutinised her face carefully. She required one hell of a job, including reshaping of her nose, chin, ears, cheekbones and upper eyelids.

'Well, your face needs a total overhaul! It will be almost impossible to do all the corrections in one sitting. Up to three surgeries may be required. But, I am not sure if you'll have the time or patience for so many procedures.'

'I am very motivated.'

I wondered whether other plastic surgeons were avoiding Chitra because of her deviant behaviour. My boss always warned me about patients with unrealistic expectations. Surgeons were also supposed to be guarded about operating on journalists, lawyers or policemen. I figured the best option would be to buy some time.

'I need to examine you thoroughly. Why don't you meet me at my clinic.'

'For the next two months, I am busy with a new project for the magazine. After that I will be after your life!' she said.

Post midnight, many moved out. Only the hardcore party animals were left behind. Some seemed drunk. We left after a while too, and on our way back, I reckoned that Nirdosh's party could turn out to be my first big break. Even if a few of these stars responded, my practice was likely to get the push start.

'I hope you had a good time,' I said to Nandini on our way back.

I was afraid that she might have felt neglected because I had done most of the talking.

'Of course it was fun. But, we should have stayed till the end!'

The next day, both of us parted ways again, courtesy our so-called glorious profession.

I started my work at the hospital with renewed energy. We often faced unique situations that were not described in the text books which were oriented to the west. These required ingenious solutions, sometimes bordering on *jugaad*. By this time, I had developed a passable fluency in Marathi and Gujarati. This enabled me to connect more effectively with patients.

Two months had passed since Nirdosh's party. There hadn't been even a single query from the celebrities I had met there. Even the much awaited call from Chitra was not forthcoming.

One weekend, there was a local conference on plastic surgery. During the lunch break, I was with a group of plastic surgeons.

Dr. Kulkarni from Thane asked me, 'So, how are you faring after the departure of Dr. Jayaraj? A number of stars live in the areas around your hospital. They must have started showing up at your clinic.'

'I am not even getting starlets, leave alone stars!'

I had laughed off his question but there was frustration on my face.

'Don't worry. Just keep on working. The trickle in your clinic will gradually become a stream.'

Kulkarni and I struck a chord. We decided to share our experiences and also assist each other whenever required.

That night, I felt like calling my parents and opening my heart to them. However, I reckoned that my dad would be shattered if he came to know that I had not made much headway. So I kept the conversation focused on Nandini, Bhavya and our relatives in Delhi.

The next day, the accountant, Dhawal showed me the monthly balance sheet of the hospital. We were in the red. I had to fix the situation quickly. There was the option of taking financial help from parents or friends, but for how long?

'Doctor, can I give you a suggestion?' Dhawal asked.

'Go ahead.'

'Hire a smart public relations guy and fete the doctors who can refer patients to you. You will soon see our turnover increasing.'

'I do not claim to be a saint. However, I have been trained in such a way that I would be very uncomfortable with all that.'

I ended the discussion but Dhawal had got me thinking. If my practice did not pick up, the only alternative left was to go back to Delhi. But I dreaded being labelled a failure.

I imagined my colleagues in Delhi saying behind my back, 'Loser, loser! This is the fate of those who try to rise too fast.'

I turned to Dr. Vidur again.

'Sir, this is Dhruv. I am in trouble.'

'Why do you call me only when the chips are down? Do you know what I have gone through in the past one month?' he grumbled.

I was facing his wrath for the first time after leaving the department, but I have to admit I loved every bit of it! It sent me back to my days of residency.

'I am sorry, sir. I was depressed. What happened to you?'

'I was diagnosed with dengue fever and admitted to the hospital for a week. Even now, I am on forced leave. Tell me about yourself.'

'I am thinking of shifting back to Delhi. Sir, you have omitted an important subject while training me.'

'What?'

'I have not been taught how to be a street smart doctor.'

'You seem to be under the illusion that success at every step is your birthright. Look at me. I have a waiting list although my practice has been built by word of mouth. I do not deny that marketing in a branch like plastic surgery is essential nowadays. You can hire a professional team to do it for you. But please do not cut corners by giving cuts. Like a long term investment, the medical practice takes time to flourish. So, stay right where you are.'

Deliberating with my guru gave me a lot of solace. But I had to sort out my financial problems before they got out of hand. The triad of friends gathered to plan a way out.

'I have a practical solution for you,' Shah said.

'Tell me fast.'

'There are a lot of gangsters in Mumbai. As a surgeon, you know the exact point where one could poke the knife or fire a shot to finish the victim in one go. You will become a prized hit man in no time!'

Shah started in a sombre tone but by the time he finished, both he and Chhatre were giggling.

'If you do not stop this monkey business, I am leaving.'

'This is the first time that I have noticed you getting irritated at our jokes. Relax. Actually, we have worked out a plan for you. The best option for you is to join a part time job at another hospital,' Shah said.

'Why so?'

'There will be two advantages.'

'I will make more money. What else?' I asked.

'You will be so busy shuttling between two hospitals that there will be no time for depression. Fatigue will help you sleep well.'

'So, you want me to do the donkey's work, like in my residency?'

'You better do it. Or else you will make an ass of yourself in this city!' Chhatre said.

Within two weeks, I found a job at Sant Ram Hospital that was conveniently situated in Vile Parle. The hospital received a lot of trauma and burn cases. As expected, it was hectic. But I felt like a real doctor, one who saved lives and limbs.

After a while, I contacted Nirdosh Khanna and requested him to let me mingle with the stars once again. I calculated that contacting more actors would increase the probability of someone responding to me. He promised to help me out.

Next day was very hectic and I reached home past midnight after operating on a factory worker who had a crush injury of the hand. There was no luxury of an off post duty. I snatched a few hours of sleep. When the alarm rang, I found it very difficult to get up. The newspaper was my best bet for switching on as there would always be some eye-popping news. But I almost froze in horror when I saw the headline. It said – 'Nirdosh Khanna - end of an era.'

The previous evening, he had been rushed to the Noble Heart Hospital after suffering a massive heart attack. Despite the doctors' best efforts, Nirdosh expired after an hour. I attended the funeral after cancelling my engagements for the day. Who's who of the industry were there. Sandhya was inconsolable. She hardly interacted with anyone. I recognized Chitra amongst the crowd. As soon as our eyes met, she rushed towards me.

'I feel like I have lost a part of myself. You must be upset too,' Chitra said, and left with a promise to see me in week's time.

Feeling forlorn, I went home. After sunset, I went to the balcony to seek comfort in the night sky. I imagined the earth as a speck in the universe and myself as a speck on the earth. However, despondency still overpowered me. I was only a master of plastic surgery, not of spirituality.

Above Average

Chitra kept her appointment with me. I gave her the last slot, so she could babble to her heart's content.

'So, you want to look as good as the divas you report about,' I asked, in an effort to understand her.

'Apart from that, I expect the reshaping to help me find Mr. Right. Maybe even get back together with my old boyfriend!' she said.

I was impressed, but also alarmed by her plain speaking.

'My bosses have taught me that treating journalists, policemen and lawyers is a pain in the neck. How do I deal with that?'

'The higher the risks you take, the bigger is the potential reward. I am sure that my looks can only get better. I promise that I will not create a ruckus if anything goes wrong.'

'Actually, even if there is a false step, we are usually able to salvage the situation. Once a complication is detected, it can be managed promptly,' I said.

I handed the mirror to her.

'Point out the features you want me to alter.'

She outlined her list. Later, her face was photographed from different angles.

'We need to have another meeting. I will make the final treatment plan after studying the photographs,' I said.

'You will not get much time, lest you develop cold feet like other surgeons.'

Immediately after she left, I started looking up the textbooks, and had discussions with other plastic surgeons. By the time she returned, the blueprint of the treatment was ready.

'If we try and do all the procedures in a single sitting, the surgery will go on for more than ten hours. Such a long surgery is only justified for a life-saving or a limb-salvage operation. I think we could work on your face in two stages. A third surgery would be required to suck out the fat from your abdomen and flanks. The fourth stage is equally important, but non-surgical. You will be given skin rejuvenation sessions.'

'What areas of the face will you cover in the first stage?'

'I will perform a rhinoplasty to thin out the tip of your nose and reduce the hump on its base. The profile will be made concave to create a feminine look. Your ears, which stick out, will be pushed back to balance the face. And I will reshape your upper eyelid to alter its hooded appearance. In the second sitting, I will make your cheekbones prominent by putting in implants. Your chin will also get an implant. For the third surgery, a thorough liposuction of the abdomen and flanks will be performed. Feel free to clarify any doubt.'

'Doc, if you go to a forest alone and are confronted by a lion, what would you do?'

'I would meekly do whatever the king of the jungle will command.'

'Similarly, I submit myself to the doctor treating me! There is no other alternative to having complete trust in your plastic surgeon. A layman's mind, however sharp it may be, can never pick up all the intricacies of the medical science.'

'I appreciate your point of view. Hospitals would be less stressful for the doctors if all patients thought like you.'

'I have always behaved well with doctors. But I can be very nasty otherwise. Why did you call me a patient? I am not sick.'

'You are not just a client anymore, but also a patient. So, I will maintain the sacred doctor-patient relationship and go that extra mile for your treatment. On the other hand, as promised, you will surrender to me unconditionally!'

We planned her surgery for two weeks later so that she had time to find a substitute at *Starsworld*. After she had left, I wondered if it was a godsent opportunity or if I had bitten off more than I could chew. I started fantasizing about making a big splash in the media with the publication of my interview in *Starsworld*.

One week passed. Pessimism was giving way to cautious optimism. However, I was hit with something else, as if a dark force was hell bent on knocking me out. I received a notice from the court, under the Consumer Protection Act. The complainant had asked for a compensation of four lakh rupees.

I remembered that one month ago I had treated a young girl, Upasna. A white patch over her right cheek had been corrected by applying a skin graft. Unfortunately, a part of the skin graft had not taken and she was left with a small, residual uncorrected patch.

During the follow up visit, I had told her, 'Do not worry. Another skin graft will do the needful.'

But the patient had turned up only after a month and that too to argue.

She had said, 'I consulted another plastic surgeon, Dr. Sanjan. He told me that he would have done a perfect job.'

The diagnosis was confirmed. Dr. Sanjan had indirectly instigated the patient's relatives with his careless comment. I had never faced any sort of litigation in my life. In panic, I rang up Dr. Rakesh, a senior surgeon at the Sant Ram Hospital and told him the long and short of it.

'I can hear the thumping of your heart through the phone! Relax. You have arrived! One is labelled a renowned doctor only if faced with a couple of Consumer Protection Act cases! It simply means you are doing a good amount of work. I will tell my lawyer to handle your case.'

I met the lawyer, Mr. Dastoor, in the evening and filled him in on all the facts.

'This case is certain to go in your favour. Partial loss of skin graft is well-known and not likely to be considered negligence.'

His assurance was a huge relief.

Just three weeks later, I got a chance to get even with Dr. Sanjan. I was visited by a middle-aged patient, a gentleman called Binod, who had been operated by Dr. Sanjan two months back. Binod had severe scarring in front of the right ear due to a road accident. To reconstruct his sidelocks, Dr. Sanjan had raised a flap of hair-bearing tissue from the scalp, rotated it and applied on the area. However, he had botched up the surgery. The direction of the hairs on the operated area was wrong. They were growing upwards. Binod was deeply distressed by his odd appearance.

'I was better off before the surgery,' he said.

'Did the doctor take the imprints of the defect while planning the case?' I asked him, to get to the heart of the matter.

'Sir, while planning, he did not foresee that on rotating the skin upside down from the donor area, the oblique slant of hair would also reverse in direction. It was as if he cooked a dish very well but spoiled it in the end by putting too much salt.'

I had an urge to give Dr. Sanjan a taste of his own medicine by suggesting the patient go for litigation. Just when I was about to speak, I remembered Dr. Vidur's teaching: 'Reveal your civilized side by rising above the primitive instinct of revenge.'

I reckoned that the vicious circle of enmity would distract me from my objective. Chitra's surgery was due in a few days and I wanted to give it my best shot.

There was no clear cut surgical solution to the problem. So, I advised the patient to use gel to modify the direction of the hair. He was convinced and went back with a smile on his face.

After the patient had left, I made a long overdue call to Dr. Vidur.

'Boss, how are you?'

'I am back in action.'

I told him about the events in the last few days. He appreciated my decision to shun rivalry and focus on my work.

Chitra was admitted a day before the surgery. She needed to be familiar with the hospital environment. When I went to her room, she told me to have a seat. Obviously, she wanted to chat.

'The thought of undergoing surgery is making me edgy,' she said.

'But, you were eagerly awaiting it.'

'I am worried about the end result. But doctor, you also look tense.'

'I am also worried about your end result!'

'So, both of us should say good luck to each other.'

'Absolutely.'

Late in the evening, I jotted down the sequence of operative steps. Dr. Kulkarni graciously agreed to join me for the surgery the next day.

As Chitra was being wheeled into the operation theatre, she was mumbling a prayer. The anaesthesia was quickly induced. Kulkarni and I got on with the job. By finishing the surgery in five hours, we prevented her from being under anaesthesia for too long.

After regaining consciousness, she was shifted to the recovery room. My body felt so stiff that I had to rest in the surgeon's room for fifteen minutes to recoup. By the time I reached the recovery room, Chitra was fully alert.

'Thanks a lot for everything. I feel only mild pain.'

By the time I came for rounds the next morning, she had been shifted to a private room. Upon entering, I was left speechless. By Chitra's side, I found Chhavi, the reigning queen of meaningful cinema. They seemed to be bosom pals because Chhavi had brought a jumbo bouquet for Chitra. Chhavi looked prettier in person than on camera. I was an avid fan and my flushed face seemed to declare this.

'Chhavi, this is the doctor responsible for my plight!'

'Actually, she has been praising you a lot. I have come to know that before you operated on her, many plastic surgeons had turned her down,' Chhavi said.

'Handling her is a tough job!' I grinned.

Chhavi looked at me intently and said, 'I have a feeling that you could play the role of a doctor on screen too.'

'I will think about it,' I replied.

I reckoned that even if I bagged the role of a doctor, I would be a sidey, unless the movie was based on a medical theme. I was beginning to make my mark. It did not make sense to waste years of training and experience on acting now.

A look at her charts revealed normal parameters. I proceeded with her first dressing. It was the moment of truth, just like lifting a maiden's veil for the first time. I was relieved because the operated areas did not reveal any nasty surprises like decreased circulation or blood collection.

After another two days in the hospital, Chitra was discharged.

Ten days later, Chitra's ears and eyelids looked distinctive in their new form. However, the persistent nasal swelling made the tip of her nose look clownish. I reassured her that her nose would look good within two weeks.

After a few days, Chitra asked for an appointment a week before her follow up date. Her subdued voice seemed like the calm before the storm. I braced myself for a possible complication or bad result. As she entered my chamber, I realized the source of her distress. Her nose, which was still a bit swollen, was the anomaly in the otherwise pleasant looking face.

'Doc, it seems that my nasal surgery has gone horribly wrong. Please do not hide anything from me,' she said.

I had faced similar situations quite often. A careless negative comment from a friend or relative made the patient believe that her new look was not likely to wow her near and dear ones. Then, the plastic surgery was thought to be an exercise in futility and the plastic surgeon perceived as a swindler!

I asked her, 'Who pointed out that your rhinoplasty has gone bad?'

'My cousin Momita told me that the swelling should have vanished by the end of the first week.'

'Is your cousin a doctor?'

'No. But her best friend got a rhinoplasty a few months ago.'

'I am sorry to say that she is not a well-wisher. Her half-baked knowledge about nose reshaping has unnecessarily upset you. Every person responds differently to surgery. In your case, it will take longer for the swelling to disappear. Your rhinoplasty went perfectly well.'

Her smile indicated that my theatrical performance had corrected her twisted thinking, at least to some extent.

By her next visit, most of the swelling had gone. A sharp nose was visible.

'You have acted like someone in early teens! So, if any problem occurs during subsequent surgeries, whose opinion would be valued more…your friends' or mine?'

'My friends'! That will give me another opportunity to fight with you. I love seeing your face turn red like an apple when you get angry.'

She continued, 'So, when are you taking me up for the next surgery?'

'Think again. Imagine that you have won a good amount of money on a television quiz show and have been given the option to leave,' I replied.

'It seems that you are still afraid of me. I know I often act a bit funny, but I am a harmless person.'

'Frankly, I am worried about the implant surgery as there is very little margin of error.'

'I trust you to give your hundred percent. So, I will be able to take any problem in my stride.'

The insertion of implants required the highest standards of sterility as even a mild infection could be disastrous. One day before Chitra's surgery, I had the operation theatre fumigated, to get rid of all the microbes. On the day of the procedure, a virtual curfew was declared in the operation area. Access was limited to those actually involved in the procedure. Murari came an hour early to ensure that everything was in perfect working order.

Until about two weeks after the surgery, I kept my fingers crossed because most of the problems declared themselves in that time. Chitra was put on strong antibiotics to prevent infection.

She came for a follow up after two weeks. Absence of swelling, redness or pain at the implant site signified a successful surgery. There had been a lot of refinement with the previous surgery. But, with the creation of prominent cheekbones and chin, her face now had an excellent feminine contour. This gave her charisma. Chitra's brand new attitude showed in her upturned nose and flirtatious gait. Her face could definitely launch a few ships, if not a thousand!

She said, 'Yes, I do love my new face, but my smile is still more or less the same.'

'The facial muscles in the skin can't be changed. Their variation is responsible for the unique expressions each of us have. But, dimples can be created.'

'Let us leave that for the future.'

I eagerly awaited the next issue of *Starsworld* as I expected to steal the limelight from the stars. As soon as I got it, I flipped to Chitra's page. There was no mention of her surgical makeover. I rang her up immediately.

'Why have you not written about your transformation brought by plastic surgery? It seems that I will always remain in the background,' I said.

'My editor rubbished the whole idea. He said that I could write about myself but only in relation to my interactions with the stars. Anyway, I have told actors close to me about my makeover and also mentioned your name to them,' she explained.

After a few days, Chitra turned up again. But the appointment was for her cousin Shagun. She had previously indicated to me that Shagun was trying to get a break in the movies and needed an important correction.

Shagun was star material. She had seductive eyes, high cheekbones and bee-stung lips. I felt that she could play a *bindaas* college girl as nicely as a village belle.

'So, Shagun, what are you up to?' I asked.

'Since I was a little girl, I have dreamed of captivating audiences on the big screen. Because of Chitra didi's persuasion, my parents have finally given their consent. To get movie ready, I have been religiously following the instructions of my physical trainer.'

'So, does Shagun have any solid offers?' I asked Chitra.

'I have already approached a few producers and directors. Shagun has got everything going for her. However, she loses out where it matters the most.'

'Tell me. I will do whatever is possible.'

'Well, Indian men have a fixation with bosoms. And she is just average in that respect. If Shagun cannot make men drool, she will not be able to make much headway in movies.'

'You have a smart plan. It is best to get the breast implants done before the debut. If one goes for it later on, somehow the whole world, including the chai walla, gets to know about it! Some inventive paparazzi even display before and after photographs to substantiate their story,' I said.

Then I turned to Shagun, 'What are your expectations?'

'Doctor, I want to look good in Indian dresses too.'

'I got it. We can position the implants towards the centre so that you look voluptuous in a choli. Is that right?'

Shagun nodded in affirmation. After examining her, I showed her all the sizers required for selecting the appropriate implant size. To my surprise, she pointed to the biggest sizer which indicated that she wanted the biggest implant.

'How greedy of her,' I thought

'Your skin will not be able to take this one. Let me decide the biggest size possible for you,' I told her.

She reluctantly agreed to my selection.

'We will get back to you in a few hours,' Chitra said and they left my office.

The same evening, I got a call from Chitra. 'Shagun is willing to undergo surgery, but wants it within three days.'

I put in the large implants so that even a dupatta couldn't hide her bust. The results were visible to Shagun as soon as she recovered from anaesthesia.

Just a few weeks after that, she came to me with a huge bouquet. Shagun had bagged a dream debut with Sethias, a top banner.

'Thanks once again. I edged out the competition, courtesy the surgical enhancement.'

'I hope that you become a superstar in Bollywood.'

After Shagun's surgery, there was no looking back. Chitra's endorsement motivated quite a few stars who had been waiting on the sidelines. The word of mouth worked slowly, but surely. Celebrities started showing up at my clinic. I left my part time job and started focusing all my energy on cosmetic surgery again.

Shaping breasts and butts became my bread and butter. The demands were mostly achievable, but sometimes outlandish. I was at my wits' end when Jahanvi, a pretty actress, wanted to be made into the most beautiful woman in the world by any means possible.

I told her, 'There may be scales for fairness and wrinkles but there is no index of beauty, or for that matter, ugliness. In fact, the idea of beauty varies not only amongst individuals but also amongst cultures. Sometimes, I come across women who look prettier to me than Miss World or Miss Universe.'

After a few counselling sessions, she realized that her demand was silly.

To share my modest success, I called my mom.

'Hi, "Mother India!" Come over to Mumbai. I promise I will make you meet your favourite stars.'

'Okay, "Mr India!" I will talk to your dad and get back to you tomorrow,' Mom replied.

The next day, Mom called as promised, 'Your dad is very keen to meet you. But he is hesitant to come to Mumbai because he is very touchy about his failure to make it to Bollywood. It will open up a lot of his old wounds.'

'Okay. Let us give him some more time to reconcile to the idea,' I said dejectedly.

The financial position of the hospital became comfortable. A few months ago, I had been passing time eating peanuts and also earned peanuts! Now, there were some days when my appointments were full. However, one thought was disturbing me. Although the stars had been very nice to me in person, I had never been invited to their private parties or premieres. I decided to point out the grave injustice to Chitra.

'Just look at the photo feature of Chintan's party in the latest issue of *Starsworld*. I gave him a facelift to make him look presentable. Every Tom, Dick and Harry is seen gyrating at his gathering, but he did not care to invite me.'

'I understand. None of the invitees are as qualified as you. But this is the way the world functions. People who are associated with mass media always have an unfair advantage. Who bothers about the level of education of Kamal Kapoor or Rizwan Khan? Take my example. I am so well known throughout the country, although my IQ must be half of yours.'

'Even that is an exaggeration!' I replied, making her laugh.

I continued, 'Anyway, I feel relieved after talking it out with you. Even I understand that an invite to me would imply that the host was utilizing my services.'

'You are absolutely right. It is quite possible that a plastic surgeon could spill the beans to the guests, especially after downing a couple of drinks. Of course, I know that you would never do that, but still, most people are sceptical.'

Just a few minutes after she had left, the phone bell rang. It was Chitra again.

'What is it? Have you forgotten your heart with me?'

'That did not happen because a few moments ago I had a thought straight from my heart. You could write about plastic surgery in magazines. That would give you the splashy image which you crave.'

'Excellent suggestion. But I entrust this job to you. Contact the editors and try to convince them to incorporate a page devoted to plastic surgery in every issue.'

'I will do so within a week,' said Chitra.

After about ten days, I received a call from her.

'Sorry Doc. I contacted two editors but both of them said that they already have columns by dermatologists and they had no immediate plans for publishing plastic surgery related material.'

I could not hide my disappointment.

'You have coaxed even the most introverted stars to come out with their secrets. Have your persuasion skills disappeared?'

'I have not given up on it. Anyway, I feel that this failure should spur you towards a bigger success. The best way to forget disappointment is to get busy with your work.'

'Please explain.'

'You have done my face nicely. Now, I need body contouring by liposuction. The bulges in my abdomen and flanks should be history!'

'I would be happy to do that because you have turned into a compliant patient.'

Soon, she was back in the hospital, which had become a second home to her. With the help of liposuction equipment, we were able to suck out about four litres of fat from her problem areas.

Immediately after regaining consciousness, she demanded to have a look at the aspirated fat.

After seeing the two jars full of yellowish liquid fat, she looked triumphant.

'So, this is the villain with whom I am constantly fighting!'

The next day, I entered Chitra's room for my rounds. Shagun was beside her. Her natural good looks had been augmented by professional make-up. The inner confidence also showed as a glow on her face. She had been in the news for getting hooked up with action hero Vikram. To my surprise, Chitra had also highlighted their hot new romance in her column.

'Hi, Doc,' Shagun said.

'You look every inch a star.'

'Thanks.'

'I thought you would bring Vikram along.'

'He is in the "just friends" category, although future promotion is not ruled out!'

'By the way, you did not even spare Shagun in your column,' I turned to Chitra.

'Doctor, you are too simple-minded. Shagun has rightly said that they are just good companions. By publicizing the so-called affair, I have killed two birds with a stone. Firstly she hogs a lot of space in the media. Secondly, it discourages the male sharks in the film industry who look at her as a delicacy!'

'Got it.'

'Doc, when will I see the final result?' Chitra asked.

'Probably in about three months. By then, most of the swelling will have gone.'

'Wow! That means I will be able to dress for the beaches.'

'The hotel pools, too!' I added.

'So what are you up to?' Shagun said to me.

'I am excited about Nandini coming back after finishing her residency. Obviously all of us will all have a get together.'

'Both of us should try to find a husband like Dr. Dhruv. When he mentioned Nandini's name, he was beaming. I am sure he will be equally attached to his children,' Chitra said to Shagun.

I commented, 'Whenever you talk to me, there is a very thin dividing line between praise and sarcasm. Anyway, I take it as a compliment. That way, I will try to live up to the image you have constructed for me.'

Moving Together

During Nandini's last visit, Mumbai had swayed sensuously to the rhythm of the monsoon. Currently, it was sulking in the hot and dry April. However, as we were moving towards our home, Nandini was the picture of gaiety. She had passed her MD and was coming back for good.

'The weather is oppressive,' I whined.

'When lovers re-unite, any season is as enchanting as the rainy season. Promise me that we will stay together for the rest of our lives,' she said and clasped my hand tightly.

'It was you who left me. Do not be tempted by some fellowship in paediatrics.'

'I am so drained; I just want to unwind for a month,' Nandini said.

I tried to avoid bringing work stresses home. But, whenever there was a complicated surgery the next day, the strain showed. That night, I was reading about the face lift surgery to be done the next morning.

'Honey, you look as tense as an exam candidate. Ease up,' Nandini said as she gently stroked my hair.

'Sometimes, stress is unavoidable. Tomorrow, I have to do a facelift on Paritosh Dubey, the veteran director. He claims that smoking sparks his creativity. Although he stopped it one week ago, there is still some risk of complications.'

'Worries overpower you because you keep holding on to them! See, just talking it out with me has made you feel so much lighter.'

'You are right.'

Nandini had planned a longish break. But the doctor in her surfaced after two weeks. She started looking for a job.

'I want to work nearby so that I do not have to spend much time commuting.'

'Why so?'

I wondered whether she had lost her ambitious streak.

'The time saved would be invested in my home and hubby.'

That day, my admiration for her grew even more.

Nandini found the job she was looking for at Sanjeevani Hospital. She had to work for about six hours a day and attend to emergencies for two days a week.

Both of us were watching a movie on television on a leisurely Sunday afternoon. When my mobile phone rang, I felt miffed at the invasion of my precious recreation time.

'Dr. Dhruv, this is Satyam. PA to Rajan ji. He wants to speak to you.'

'Okay, please give the phone to him.'

'Good afternoon doctor. I need to see you soon,' he said in his unique voice.

Rajan's last two movies had flopped. But he had bounced back from even bigger professional setbacks.

I did some quick thinking and replied, 'It would be better if I come to your home or office.'

A star with such a massive fan following could have caused a minor riot at our small hospital.

'That is better. You will be my honoured guest. Satyam will finalize the details with you.'

I fixed up the consultation for Tuesday evening. Full of self-admiration, I bragged to Nandini, 'See, even Rajan wants to be operated by me. I am going to be the don of my speciality.'

'That calls for a celebration. *Aata kya Khandala*?' Nandini said and we set off on a drive to the Western Ghats.

Satyam came to fetch me at the appointed time.

'Welcome doctor. I have heard a lot about your skills,' Rajan said.

Rajan's well preserved face indicated that he was no stranger to plastic surgery! The voice which enthralled millions was very distinctive, just like his light grey eyes.

'Rajan ji, there are many plastic surgeons who are senior to me. Then, why did you choose me?'

'Medical science is advancing rapidly. A younger surgeon is likely to have more expertise in the newer techniques,' he said.

Unlike most Indians, who express themselves using their hands, he used his face.

'Rajan ji, what is your concern?'

'Doctor, you must be aware that Rizwan Khan and Kamal Kapoor have overtaken me. Ever since my last two movies bombed, I have felt vulnerable in this dog eats dog world of Bollywood.'

'You think that a change in your appearance could work for you?'

'My hairy chest, often referred to as a Persian carpet, was the symbol of masculinity in the nineties. Nowadays, stubble is cool but body hair is out. It is easy to update the wardrobe but coping with the changing body fashions is so tough! I cannot do the rigorous workouts which my trainer has advised. Use a short cut to make an Adonis out of me!'

I examined him and worked out a plan for him in a jiffy.

'Your female fans adore you unconditionally! Still, there is no harm in keeping up with the times. You already have a well-toned chest and abdomen. All that needs to be done is selective liposuction of some areas. That will create the impression of a six pack abdomen. Then, you will look for excuses to remove your shirt!'

'Smart plan. What about body hair? Waxing is like third degree torture.'

'Lasers for permanent hair reduction are already being used abroad. In just a matter of months, they will be introduced in the Indian market.'

'Thanks Doc. I will be in touch with you soon.'

By the time the meeting had finished, it was dark. While on my way back, I was planning the logistics for Rajan's surgery. When I reached home, I hugged Nandini tightly and lifted her up.

'Everything is on track. He should be on my operating table within a few days.'

'I am proud of you. And your tricks to create illusions!' Nandini said.

Next day, as soon as I reached my hospital, I called for Murari.

'We will soon be operating upon film star Rajan. Where should we plan the surgery, considering the privacy issue?'

'Doctor sahib, you are right. This is a special situation and we might have to look for a place away from our hospital. The other alternative is to operate at night. Give me some time. By tomorrow morning, I will come up with a concrete strategy.'

I got the much-awaited call from Rajan that evening itself.

'Thanks once again for your advice. I have come to the conclusion that it would be almost impossible to remain hidden while getting plastic surgery in India. So, I will fly to the US for a supposed holiday, but actually to get the liposuction. After a few months, my public relations team will circulate a story about the transformation of my physique because of extensive workouts! I too will give interviews in the media about my fitness *fundas*!'

'You are revealing all your trade secrets to me.'

'I am opening up to you because I feel that you will maintain confidentiality. Bye.'

Nandini guessed something had happened from my sullen expression.

'What is it? Has Rajan decided to ditch you?'

'Yes, I am feeling hurt because he used me. He probably already had plans to get his surgery done abroad. Luckily, I did not talk about his surgery with any other hospital staff except Murari.'

'There are so many patients who take your opinion and get operated elsewhere. Why have you taken this episode to heart?'

'I feel like someone who had to turn back a few steps from the summit of Mount Everest.'

'Come on! There is a huge world beyond Rajan,' Nandini said and took me in her arms.

'The world enclosed within your arms is enough for me!' I whispered and she hugged me tighter.

I started meeting my friends Chhatre and Shah quite often as Nandini got along well with their wives. I noticed that she loved to cuddle their kids. Obviously she was pining for a little one of her own.

I also planned to introduce Nandini to Chitra. My only worry was that she could misread Chitra's wisecracks. Before I could ring her up, Chitra contacted me.

'Hi. Three months have passed since the liposuction. The swelling has subsided and I am happy with my overall shape. But, a depression has appeared in a small area, just below the belly button. I will show you tomorrow.'

'Let us not jump to any conclusions before I examine you. See you at eleven in the morning.'

Her call set alarm bells ringing in my mind. I suspected that there was some real issue because Chitra had become a seasoned patient. I was also afraid that her unique relationship with me could become strained.

She had judged correctly. In my effort to flatten the area as much as possible, I had overdone the liposuction. A depression had appeared in an area of around two inches in diameter. Since the swelling had gone away completely, there were no chances of spontaneous improvement.

'Your concern is justified. While taking out your fat, I was too greedy!' I confessed.

'Now what?' she asked pensively.

'I can easily fix your problem. Under local anesthesia, fat will be aspirated from the inner thighs and injected into the depressed area to fill it up. The result will show immediately,' I said.

'A few months ago, you told me that I was entering your plastic surgery club and exit out of it was very difficult. I thought it was a joke. But that seems to be true.'

'That was actually said in jest only. Tomorrow itself, we will post you for the touch up surgery so that you start feeling good soon.'

Next day, we did the transfer from one account to another. The fat was sucked out from the inner portion of her thighs.

After purification, it was injected into the deficient area. Post surgery, I showed the result to her.

'Let us hope that the injected fat stays.'

'I have done a bit of overcorrection. So, even if there is mild fat absorption, your look will be maintained.'

'Thanks, as always. So, when am I meeting Nandini?'

'Within a few days.'

At home, Nandini and I discussed the day's happenings.

'Today, I did a touch up surgery on Chitra, the chief columnist of *Starsworld*. I had previously performed three plastic surgeries on her. We will have a get-together with her as well as her cousin Shagun.'

'Dhruv, I understand that having ravishing ladies as clients is a part of your profession. Still, sometimes I do feel insecure. Although this amounts to doubting your love for me, I cannot help it. It is only you who can make me come to terms with it.'

'I might feel the same since some of your colleagues are handsome hunks. Let us promise each other that we will not fool around.'

'I feel so relieved after talking it out with you. Actually, my friends have been telling me that all husbands were to be thought of as guilty of cheating on their wives until proved otherwise! I have also been advised to keep a check on you by making frequent calls on your mobile.'

'You are safe. I don't require surveillance.'

'Dhruv, tomorrow is an important day in our lives.'

'It is neither an anniversary nor a birthday. What is it about?'

'Silly! Have you ever thought about an addition to the family?'

'I have been working hard to make it happen! But ultimately it is God's gift.'

'I missed my periods. I will get the pregnancy test tomorrow, but a baby seems to be on the way.'

'Why didn't you tell me before?'

'Wanted to give you a surprise.'

The next morning, I went to my office but my mind was stuck on Nandini's report. Around noon, I got the much awaited call.

'Yes! The test is positive. This is the best gift I have got from you so far.'

'You are always welcome. But actually, you should be thanking the champion sperm who won the race amongst a million contestants.'

'Shut up. I know the physiology of reproduction better than you. Come back soon,' Nandini said.

As I reached home, instead of hugging me, Nandini leaned against my shoulder. She seemed to be saying that she needed my support as much as my love.

I announced the good news to family members. Our parents seemed even more ecstatic than us and offered to come over.

Initially, she did have occasional bouts of nausea and vomiting. But after about three months, she started feeling a lot better.

It had been a while since I had talked to Chitra. Just when I started feeling sulky, she called.

'Hi! You must be feeling like punching me. So, I will tell you something which will make you smile.'

To heighten the suspense, she paused for a while and then said, 'I have found my beau, thanks to you.'

'I am delighted. Describe your victim in detail!'

'Come on. Get over your jealousy! Sarjeevan is madly in love with me. He is a publisher. To be honest, he is most attracted to those features of mine which you created.'

'So, we do make real difference in the lives of people. I am so happy for you. Do come over to our place and bring Shagun along.'

'There is no need to use me as a tool to reach Shagun. You can call her directly.'

Chitra and Shagun did make a surprise visit after two days.

'We have come to mingle with your lovely wife and not to listen to your worthless talk! By the way, what have you done to earn her?' Chitra asked.

'I did a lot of good deeds in my previous life,' I said, to Nandini's delight.

Vastly outnumbered by the fairer sex, I beat a hasty retreat and let the three of them carry on the conversation. After they had left, I asked Nandini her opinion regarding my loyal clients.

'Chitra chirps a lot but seems to be good at heart. Shagun looks so angelic that if I were a man, I would have lost my bearings. So I do appreciate you for resisting women and remaining loyal to me.'

'By the way, these damsels are chased by stylish studs and a boring doctor like me is unlikely to excite them. So, you are safe!'

During the fourth month of Nandini's pregnancy, our gynaecologist advised us to undergo an ultrasound to rule out any birth defects. The night before the scan, a sound awakened me. I struggled to open my eyes. It was Nandini. She was coming out of the washroom.

'What is it, honey? Are you okay?' I said.

'I have not been able to sleep even for a moment.'

'I know you are worried about the scan.'

'As a child specialist, I have seen so many babies with birth defects. I would be devastated if my child is born abnormal.'

'Come on! You counsel so many parents. Still, you are thinking negatively. Major anomalies are extremely rare. It is highly unlikely that our child will have a birth defect.'

I stroked her gently for a while and soon she went to sleep.

In the morning, the worry reappeared.

The ultrasonologist said, 'Too much knowledge can be as dangerous as too little knowledge! That's why doctors usually make poor patients.'

After the scan, the smile was back on Nandini's face as the report was normal. From then on, it was smooth sailing. Her mom arrived two weeks before the expected delivery date.

The labour pains started three days earlier than the expected date and culminated in a normal delivery.

'It is a healthy baby girl,' Dr. Rekha, the senior gynaecologist, announced.

'Are you happy?' Nandini asked me when I went to see her. She was aware that North Indians craved a male child.

'Of course, I am elated. Times are changing. To me a girl is as precious as a boy.'

I hugged her. Then, I experienced the supreme bliss of holding one's child for the first time.

'Who does she resemble?' Nandini asked the usual question.

'Right now, the little one has lot of swelling on her face. In a couple of days, her features will be better defined.'

Both of us had already decided on names for a boy as well as a girl. We named her Saloni, to rhyme with Nandini.

The mother and the baby both were discharged three days later.

'So, what do you feel about her looks now?'

Like most mixed race children, Saloni had a striking appearance. She had inherited the soft facial contours of her mother while the long forehead and dimpled chin were on me. But, I was in a mood to tease Nandini.

'There has been a good combining of genes. So her looks are an almost equal blend of both parents. But the poor little thing will ultimately need a correction of her pug-nose and prominent ears,' I said, with a straight face.

'Shut up and keep your plastic surgery to yourself! At least, spare your daughter,' Nandini said angrily.

'In mammals, mothers become super aggressive if they perceive even the slightest danger to their offspring,' I gestured to my mother-in-law.

'Human females are volatile with or without a cub!' Nandini laughed, after getting my joke.

Baywatch and Bollywood

Just a few days after the arrival of Saloni, there was another reason for euphoria. Dr. Palmer, my American guru, came to Mumbai to attend the annual conference of Plastic Surgery Association of India. He visited my centre. I amused him by recounting the interesting incidents at my hospital. But he made me laugh even more by digging into the humorous stories of Lakeview Hospital.

'A fundamental change is taking place in the mindset of the public. Many seek procedures which are less invasive, even if the improvement is less dramatic. Instant gratification with nil or minimum downtime is the new mantra. So, you have lunch time skin polishing and before party laser facials. Get yourself upgraded for exciting new technologies like lasers, Botulinum toxin injections, fillers, etc. I foresee that these procedures will become commonplace,' Dr. Palmer said.

'Got your point. I have become complacent. A thirty-five-year-old man is acting like a retired person. But, you are a young man at sixty-five years.'

'Not a young man, but a boy! I still look forward to life, not down upon it,' he grinned.

'Your joie de vivre is infectious.'

'Medical technology is advancing incredibly fast. The gains in the next ten or twenty years could be much more than what we achieved in the last century,' he said.

'The mother of all breakthroughs will be the taming of ageing. That would lead to a re-appraisal of all our philosophies and beliefs,' I added.

'It might be possible to prevent ageing at the cellular level. However, to reverse changes in already aged cells is likely to remain in the realm of science fiction. So, for people of my age, there is not much hope.'

'Which place are you exploring after the conference?' I asked.

'I will be in the Western Ghats for a bird-watching trip. By my next visit, I would like you to have a full-fledged aesthetic centre with lasers, skin polishing and other facilities.'

Initially, I took Dr. Palmer's idea of setting up a laser clinic with a pinch of salt. The aesthetic lasers were in the initial stages of clinical use and had not stood the test of time. They were also insanely expensive. I had a feeling that lasers could also meet a fate like some other technologies which could not withstand rigorous medical scrutiny. After their last rites, they were resting peacefully in the old and dusty issues of journals on the shelves of medical libraries!

But the thought stuck because a new venture was just the right prescription for putting life in the fast lane again. I put up the idea to Nandini to gauge her opinion.

She said, 'Smart man! You have found an easy way to increase the number of pretty ladies in your clinic. That would mean there is a higher likelihood of you going astray.'

'Nandini, please be serious. We have to make a decision fast.'

Her voice became resolute.

'No second thoughts. We are going through with this project. If you fall short of funds, just dip into my pockets.'

'That is awesome.'

As soon as Saloni was forty days old, all of us came to Delhi to seek the blessings of her grandparents. Dad's eyes became moist after holding his granddaughter. For the next three days, he spent a lot of time with Saloni and even babbled like a kid.

I also visited Dr. Vidur to get his views on venturing into aesthetic lasers. We spent an evening together at his house.

I explained my plan to him.

'As always, my blessings are with you.'

I set about getting a hang of the new technologies. Hands-on training sessions were being organized at various conferences. Dermal fillers would diminish wrinkles instantly. With Botulinum toxin injections, the results appeared in about a week. When both were combined, the face looked as if it had been ironed!

In one such meeting at Pune, my friend, Dr. Santosh and I were attending a demo on fillers and Botulinum toxin injections.

Dr. Kim Lee, a lovely lady doctor from Singapore had been flown in as the clinical instructor.

I said to Prashant, the organizer, 'Tell me something about Kim.'

'She did her MBBS from Singapore and then concentrated on cosmetology. After training overseas for two years, she set up her aesthetic clinic at Singapore. Because of good stage presence, she is in demand all over the world as an instructor.'

'Interesting. Most of the doctors who are listening to her are senior to her and more qualified, too. But, just four years after finishing her MBBS, Kim has an enviable career and lifestyle.'

We had presumed that the organizers would arrange some volunteers. To our surprise, Dr. Kim Lee asked for volunteers from amongst the attending doctors. I noticed Santosh's face glow with excitement. Without even looking at me, he made a dash towards the stage.

'Doctor Kim, I have had very prominent horizontal forehead lines for a long time. This is a family trait.'

'Sure. You are a good candidate to show the instant result of fillers.'

Within seconds, doctors from the audience surrounded Dr. Kim and Dr. Santosh. As the injections were given, they tried to pick up the technique by constantly questioning Dr. Kim. Santosh's forehead looked decidedly smoother at the end of the session.

'As soon as you reach home, Pushpa is going to hug you really tight. I am worried that you may faint because of suffocation!' I said.

'Let us see what happens. Actually, as Dr. Kim was calling for volunteers, it suddenly occurred to me that I should give Pushpa a surprise.'

I called him up the following evening.

'How are you doing?'

'I am fine otherwise. There is no swelling or redness.'

'What do you mean by otherwise?'

'Despite saying sorry umpteen times, Pushpa is not talking to me. She said she did not like such nasty surprises and that my previous look was more distinctive.'

'But, you have a way out. In ten months, your face will go back to normal.'

After four days, I got another call from Santosh.

'Pushpa has done a volte face. She has started liking my face and wants me to continue with the filler injections.'

'The moral of the story is that whenever Santosh leaves home, he is on parole!'

After observing the wonder of the injections, I turned my attention to lasers. After I had made a query, the salesmen of the laser distributors would appear in no time, as if they were using Star Trek teleportation. Each one made such an impressive presentation that you felt like writing a cheque immediately. But Sanjay Kumar, from Trulight Lasers, was the most articulate as well as persistent. As usual, I expressed my reservations to him.

'I do not think that I have enough clients to make the project economically viable.'

'Sir, can I ask you a question?'

'Yes, go on.'

'Who came first, the chicken or the egg?'

'This question has puzzled humans since ages and is still as confusing.'

'But one thing is sure. If one out of these is there, the other is likely to come.'

'Agreed.'

'So, if you buy my machine, it will definitely attract clientele who require laser.'

That statement proved to be the clincher for the sale. The laser was to be shipped in about a month. A token advance was paid. The amount to be financed turned out to be reasonable because Nandini loaned me most of her savings. That was the best loan deal one could get. It was without any collateral, interest free, and could be defaulted upon without any fear of litigation

Saloni's first birthday was near. She had become our focus. Whenever I returned home, Nandini would excitedly tell me about her latest milestone.

I said to Nandini, 'We should have a grand birthday celebration for her.'

'You are no different from those *Punjus* who take loans for gaudy celebrations. We will have a party at home with a few close friends.'

'Instead of being a showman, I will be your yes man and shall do as you please, princess!'

'Oh Dhruv, you make me so happy just with the way you talk!'

Two days before Saloni's birthday, I had to operate on Anjali, the actress who had ended her movie career to become a homemaker. After two pregnancies in rapid succession, her lower abdominal skin had lost its tone and was hanging like an apron. She was in for a tummy tuck.

Anjali's surgery went according to plan. The excess fat and skin, worthless before and even more so after removal, were consigned to the dustbin. The rest of the skin was pulled downwards while the belly button was given a new position. The lax underlying muscles were tightened with the help of stitches. Closure was done with staples.

Two days later, I started my morning round from Anjali's room. She seemed comfortable. I instructed my junior, Dr. Sujay, to do her dressing in the evening and inform me about the condition of the operative site.

Back home, Nandini made me run around on various errands. Mom had come all the way from Delhi just to be with her little darling on the special day.

In the evening, just after the guests had started arriving, I got a call from Dr. Sujay.

'Sir, I opened Anjali's dressing. About one inch wide portion of the skin appears blackish. I have not told her anything as yet. It will be better if you assess the case,' Sujay said.

'Okay, I will check the dressing tomorrow morning. Meanwhile, tell her to take a lot of fluids and put her on a Lomodex-40 drip,' I instructed.

When Sujay hung up the phone, the chatter of guests started sounding jarring.

It took Nandini only a few minutes to judge my state of mind.

'What is it honey? Some crisis at the hospital?'

I told her everything.

'Oh god! Why did this have to happen today? This profession really sucks.'

Both of us feigned smiles for the guests. We did not want to spoil the day for the others. Shagun did point out that I was listless. I attributed it to fever and body ache. After the celebration ended, I had a sleepless night. My brain was working at a maniacal pace to understand the cause of the disaster.

I opened Anjali's dressing the next day. Part of the skin was devoid of its blood supply. I remembered a line from a plastic surgery textbook; 'Plastic surgery is a battle between beauty and blood supply.'

I told Anjali, 'We will have to operate you again to remove the dead skin. That will be in about a week's time.'

Surprisingly, she took it very sportingly. But I had to get to the bottom of it. Discussions with a few colleagues were not helpful. Sujay and I sat down for a brainstorming session and went through her file and other clinical records. All blood investigations were normal. Clinical notes by Sujay indicated no significant abnormality. There had been no episodes of low blood pressure during the surgery

The next day, I found Murari waiting for me in my office.

'Sir, I have valuable information for you. Anjali madam has been discreetly chewing tobacco, in the form of *Gutkha*, even after the surgery. It would have gone unnoticed but for the sweeper who discovered pouches of it in the rubbish collected from her room.'

'Thanks Murari ji. Your contribution to this hospital will be written in golden letters.'

The puzzle had been solved. She had been chewing tobacco to ward off post surgical stress. Her sister, who had been staying with her, chose to keep mum, probably on Anjali's insistence. The contraction of the small blood vessels, triggered by tobacco, decreased the blood supply to the skin edges.

But where did we go wrong? I again called for the file. In the column where addictions are to be mentioned, was written; 'No addiction.' I immediately called for Sujay.

'Why the hell did you choose not to record that she was a tobacco addict?' I shouted.

Sujay was stunned because he had never seen me so agitated.

'Sir, I enquired regarding smoking or alcohol intake. But it never occurred to me that a renowned actress, married into a prestigious family, could be chewing tobacco.'

'The whole world is not stagnant like your small town. In Mumbai, ladies are neck and neck with men in every sphere, including vices!'

I did not fire Sujay as he was otherwise a sincere and hardworking doctor. He had made an error of judgment, but had not been willfully negligent.

Confronting Anjali was the next step.

'You have spared no effort to spoil your surgery!'

'Oh! I am so sorry. It never occurred to me that chewing Gutkha would have an effect on my healing after the surgery.'

'From now on, even if you chew a single pouch, I will discharge you immediately,' I thundered.

After I reached home, I realized that I had made Sujay a scapegoat. After all, I too had failed to enquire about Anjali's addictions properly during the pre-operative consultation.

After her revision surgery, we were able to give Anjali a decent result. The episode made me realize that even minor oversights could prove costly for the patient. Doctors had to strive for a zero error approach.

Meanwhile, Shagun's latest release, *Nayi Subah*, was raking in the moolah at the box office. Taking her success as my own, I called her up.

'Well done Shagun. I saw your movie in a multiplex. Even there, a few people whistled at your raunchy dance number. But your acting was also notable. The critics would be forced to sit up and take notice.'

'Thanks. The critics have also noticed a big flaw in me. I will tell you the details at our next meeting.'

Shagun came the very next day. To my utter surprise, she had brought two movie glossies.

'As I hinted, I am still not over my teething troubles. Look at the centre spread of Nonita in a red bikini. She oozes sheer oomph.'

After that, she showed me an article from another magazine. 'Now, read this. I lost the role in *Saagar Kinare* to Nonita because I have never appeared in a two piece bikini, not even in a photo shoot.'

'What is stopping you?'

'The bulges in my inner thighs and flanks. They are so stubborn! Refuse to melt with even the most strenuous workout.'

I examined her and said, 'You require liposuction. There will be no visible scars or big incisions. Within three months, you will be a photographer's delight.'

'Oh Doc, I would worship you if you give me the figure of a Bond girl!'

'Then why delay? Exchange the shooting dates for surgery dates.'

Within a week, Shagun was on the operation table. I introduced the liposuction tubes through tiny incisions placed in inconspicuous positions and dealt with the fat. Postoperatively, she was given elastic garments for an early resolution of the swelling.

Shagun came for her follow up visit three months later, bringing another magazine with her.

'What is it now?'

'Relax! I have not come with a complaint. Just have a look at this.'

Shagun showed her pictures which had been shot at a beach resort in Goa. She sizzled in a black bikini.

'Your figure is now on a par with the *Baywatch* girls!' Keep it up.'

'Doc, you are my best kept secret.'

A month later, I found Nonita knocking at my door. As she settled in my office, I wondered what could be offered to the perfect ten.

'Doctor, I want to have a washboard stomach.'

'From your pictures in movie magazines, it appears there is not even an extra ounce of abdominal fat.'

She smiled, 'I deliberately push in my abdomen during the shoots. Actually, there is a minor bulge which needs to go.'

Suddenly, I realized that by treating her, I risked boycott by Shagun. So, I told Nonita to call me in a day.

After she had gone, I called Shagun.

'Your number one competitor, Nonita came today. She wants me to contour her abdomen.'

I did not say anything further and put the ball in her court.

'Go ahead. I have got over my body insecurity. In fact, three contestants from last year's Miss India pageant have bagged roles in movies. In the future, having a gorgeous figure will be the key to gain entry into films as lead actresses.'

Conned

I received a communication from Trulight Lasers. It stated that my laser machines were arriving in a few days. This was a signal to plan for the inauguration. I called upon Sanjay Kumar, the company executive, to guide me again.

'Sir, it has to be a grand show. We will have a big invitation list so that maximum people can get a glimpse of the lasers. A press conference as well as an effective ad campaign will add to our visibility.'

'Can we do without the ads?'

'You better get rid of your inhibitions. Aesthetic clinics advertise all over the world, and in future, it may become common in India too. We are not going to put you on the billboards with a hat like Uncle Sam's and the catchphrase: "Dr. Dhruv needs you!" The ads will be framed according to the guidelines of the Maharashtra Medical Council.'

'What about the chief guest for the inauguration?'

'Preferably, it should be an actress or a model, to communicate that we stand for elegance and beauty.'

'Okay. Leave that part to me.'

It took me just a few seconds to decide the chief guest. It had to be Shagun.

She readily agreed.

On the inauguration day, I had first-hand experience of Shagun's magnetism. As long as she was there, all eyes were on her. The clever girl was doing her own branding too. She was wearing a sari with the pink, backless blouse which had become as big a hit as the movie *Pyaar Vyaar* in which she had worn it. The invitees paid attention to the lasers only after she and her blouse were gone.

From day one, clients trickled into the aesthetic centre. They were probably curious about the novel technology which promised to solve hitherto unmanageable problems like unwanted hair and birthmarks. However, most of them did not get laser procedures done as they were probably waiting for others to try them out first! Suspicions about the possible adverse effects and effectiveness persisted, even after thorough counselling.

However, a few brave souls did take the plunge and our lasers started being used. But it led to the proverbial end of innocence. A simple knife wielding surgeon had become an entrepreneur, albeit a reluctant one. Nandini went to the extent of calling me a bluff master!

One month after the inauguration, I happened to read an advertisement in the newspaper regarding a laser clinic. To my horror, the machine was of the same make as mine and the clinic was in my neighbourhood. Dr. Sandhya had probably ordered the laser a few days after my installation of it. I was distraught as I had a competitor right next door, whereas I had been expecting a free run in my locality for at least a few years.

At our monthly adda, I discussed the predicament with my friends Chhatre and Shah.

'My neighbour could make a big dent in my laser practice. I never imagined that she could buy the expensive equipment.'

'You cannot escape competition in the aesthetic field because everyone is trying to jump into it. Healthy competition is actually the best antidote to complacency,' Chhatre said.

'Actually, I am jittery because I have invested money beyond my means.'

Determined to put my best foot forward, I adopted the patient-centric approach in the aesthetic centre. The staff was told to keep in mind the line – 'The customer is the queen!'

The interaction with the clients in the first month provided a window to the aesthetic aspirations of Indian women. The first and the foremost was fairness. About one-third of the ladies were regularly using fairness creams, because they equated fair with lovely.

Kanchan, a girl with attractive features, came in for a fairness fix.

Her mother told me, 'Doctor sahib, we are looking for a match for her. But, many good proposals have been lost because of her dark complexion. Please do something for her.'

'What treatments has she had so far?'

'Doctor, let me tell you. Fairness creams are okay, but I hate it when my Mom forcibly rubs lemon and other fruits on my cheeks. Sometimes, there is irritation and burning of the skin,' Kanchan interrupted.

'She has got a flawless skin. Why don't you leave her alone?'

'Doctor sahib, what do we do? The attitude of society cannot be changed overnight.'

'Our skin colour depends on the concentration of cells called melanocytes. That is basically inherited from our parents.

The maximum change in skin tone possible by using fairness creams or medicines is one or two shades. This can be achieved otherwise also by sun avoidance and by using sunscreen,' I explained.

But their blank expression showed that my explanation went over their heads. Or perhaps, it was not what they wanted to hear.

'But I have heard that lasers can do the job.'

'Even with lasers, I cannot promise a major change in skin colour.'

It was quite likely that they would try out more clinics and ultimately be allured with a false assurance by some crafty practitioner.

After I came out of the office, I gazed at the images of the deities put up in the waiting area. Apart from Lord Krishna and Shiva, all the gods and goddesses were shown as extremely fair. It seemed that white complexion was also worshipped!

The other major concern was hair. This was beautifully summed up by a starlet Aini, who visited the centre within a few days.

'Doctor, I have a major defect. The hair I want is thinning while the unwanted hair is increasing! Please get me out of this mess.'

'Relax. You have not been singled out. This is a common problem. We will treat the unwanted hair with laser sessions. For your scalp hair growth, lotions and oral medicines will be prescribed.'

Another lady, Rameeta, went a step further.

'Doctor, give me a strong drug so that all body and facial hair is finished off in one go,' she said.

'But such a medicine would also destroy scalp hair. Drugs are not so smart as yet,' I replied.

'Doesn't matter. I will wear a wig!' she answered and both of us burst into laughter.

To resolve other hairy issues, I also started hair transplant, the plastic surgery which comes closest to farming.

The first case was Dr. Saraf, a psychiatrist, who had tremendous faith in me because I had already operated on him twice. Dr. Kulkarni and his team came to help me out. We harvested a strip from the back of the head and then divided it into hundreds of grafts comprising one or two follicles. The grafts were handled very carefully. Then, they were implanted in the bald area.

The postoperative result was satisfactory as Dr. Saraf got a hairline in the front.

'So, how do you feel now?' I asked him expectantly.

Saraf replied, 'You have converted a bald chicken into one with a crown!'

He was referring to his thin face with its disproportionately long nose.

'Thanks to stem cell technology, hair transplants may become unnecessary in future. It is likely to be written about as another chapter of medical history,' I remarked.

Shagun too came to avail the services of the centre she had inaugurated. She wanted a laser photo-facial for glowing skin. I started the treatment immediately. After the session, she looked at herself in the mirror.

Suddenly, she made a horrific expression and said, 'Doc, where has my mole gone?'

'Before starting the treatment, I had noticed a mole on the chin, but there is no reason why it should vanish,' I replied.

'Actually it was an artificial mole, created by a tattoo artist!'

'If you had told me before starting the treatment, I would have covered it with a tape. The laser has zapped it. It spares a natural mole. Get it redone after a few days.'

The new ventures ate into most of my leisure time. But I made it a point to watch the movies which starred my patients. *Rafta Rafta* starring Madhurima hit the theatres about two months after she met me. Although I hadn't heard from her since her consultation with me, I related to her.

'I am concerned about the flaring of my nostrils,' she had told me during her first meeting with me.

'The only procedure you require is shaping of the base of your nose. The excess nostril skin will be trimmed and the rest will be turned inwards, bringing it in a better position,' I proposed.

'Could you show me the expected result?'

'Sure. Just wait for a while.'

I morphed her photograph on the computer and then called her in.

'Check the before and after photos on the computer screen.'

She looked at the pictures and said, 'Could my nose be made narrower?'

'Technically speaking, that is not possible and could even compromise your breathing.'

'Thanks for your attention. I will get back to you soon.'

However, she did not turn up again, and I presumed that she had gone doctor shopping.

While watching the movie, I noticed that her nose was not the same as when I had seen it in my clinic. During a song, she lifted up her nose and the camera closed in. That was enough for me to pick up the otherwise inconspicuous rhinoplasty incision lines at the bases of both nostrils.

To my utter surprise, she reappeared in my clinic a few days later.

'Good to see you again. How did your rhinoplasty go?' I asked, wanting to embarrass her.

'It must be Shagun. I had told her not to disclose my surgery to you. But she seems to be staunchly loyal to you,' she said.

'Actually, I got a hint while watching your latest movie.'

'To tell you the truth, I went to Dr. Prakhar for a second opinion. He also showed me the before and after photos on a computer, but with as much correction as I wanted. So, I got my surgery done the next day. But, the actual result was even less than what you had shown me. He has advised a re-operation. But I want you to do it. I hope you are not angry with me for ditching you.'

'Not at all. Filmy folks have taught us not to think of anyone as a permanent friend or enemy!'

'Does that mean you will take me up for the touch up surgery?'

'If Madhurima requests, even angels cannot refuse, leave alone a lowly doctor like me.'

Her surgery went well. However, Madhurima seemed bothered during her last follow up visit, although her nose looked perfect.

'Doctor, I have come to know you are doing plastic surgery on a struggling actress to make her resemble me!' she said.

I was about to burst into laughter but restrained myself, lest she be offended.

'I swear that nothing like that is going on. Anyway, it is technically impossible to alter someone to make them an exact copy of someone else. But, I do need to know about the source of the rumour.'

'Chitra told me.'

'You know very well that Chitra is a prankster.'

'At first, I also thought that she was pulling a fast one on me. However, Chitra told me that she had seen this actress at your clinic a few days ago.'

'The last time she herself visited the clinic was about two months ago.'

'Doc, I am sorry for acting so dumb. Please do not talk about this with anybody!'

'Okay. But, whenever I need to smile, I will think of it.'

After Madhurima had left, I connected to Chitra.

'You have crossed all limits. Madhurima was a nervous wreck when she came to me.'

'It was typical attention seeking behaviour! You have not called me for so long. As for Madhurima, she invited it on herself because she played a nasty prank on me on April Fool's Day.'

'I did not contact you because I wanted to give you and Sarjeevan some space,' I said.

'Doc, our special relationship is unshakeable. Sarjeevan is the love of my life, but you are my confidante.'

New aesthetic clinics were mushrooming in anticipation of the expected boom in cosmetology and cosmetic surgery. I happened to find an unusually big ad about the inauguration of a hospital in Bandra by the name of Arpit Cosmetic Surgery Centre.

After about a week, Dr. Jayaraj called me from Dubai.

'Hi Dhruv. Please do me a favour. Dr. Arpit, my friend's son, has started plastic surgery practice in Bandra. He will require your guidance in difficult cases.'

'Where did he train for plastic surgery?' I asked out of curiosity.

'Well, after doing MBBS and MS from India, he obtained M.Ch. in plastic surgery from Moldavia. After that, he came to

Dubai to work with me. I have tried my best to hone his skills. But the time was too short because he was in a hurry to establish his hospital.'

The fact that he had earned his plastic surgery degree from an obscure place in Europe made me uneasy. Dr. Jayaraj was trying to promote a doctor whose credentials were in the grey zone. But the burden of his favours to me proved too weighty and I had to overrule my conscience.

All I could say was, 'I will do whatever I can. Just tell him to contact me.'

Dr. Arpit called me after a few minutes, probably to ensure that I would not backtrack. He invited me to his hospital.

As soon as I entered his centre, I was flabbergasted by the great attention to detail. The reception area had ultra-modern interiors while the pretty receptionists were wearing designer uniforms. The operation theatres were also state of the art. By raising the bar, the guy was forcing mediocre doctors like me to catch up.

Arpit came to the point. 'Sir, I would need your help in difficult or complicated cases. Jayaraj uncle told me that you are the only surgeon who he can vouch for.'

'I appreciate Dr. Jayaraj for being so confident about me,' I said gleefully. Who doesn't like praise?

I continued, 'Normally, I do not operate on plastic surgery cases outside my hospital. But this is like a sister concern. Be assured of my full support.'

'With your kind permission, can we put your name as a visiting consultant?'

'Sure,' I said. There was no other choice as I could not renege on the promise I had made to Dr. Jayaraj.

It was not long before I got a call from Arpit. He requested me to do a breast reduction surgery. Upon reaching his centre, I was taken towards the operation theatre complex immediately. However, the patient's husband stopped us on the way.

'Yes, how can we help you?' Arpit asked.

'Doctor, I have a small request. Please ensure that my wife's breasts look like they did when she was a newly married girl!'

'We will try our best. However, it is impossible to make her breasts like those of a young lady's in all aspects,' I explained.

'Just ignore this crazy man,' Arpit whispered to me and we moved on.

An assistant handed the operation theatre dress to me. I was surprised to see a label with my name written in bold letters. I proudly put on my personalized dress and entered the pre-operative room.

Dr. Arpit and I examined the lady and I was introduced by name to the patient. I felt relieved that I would not be a phantom surgeon.

'Why do you want your breasts to be reduced,' I asked the patient, a middle-aged house wife.

'The main reason is the discomfort in the neck and the shoulders due to the weight of the breasts and the pressure they put on my bra straps. Of course, I also want them to be lifted because they have sagged a lot.'

'You will get a good shape but there will be a vertical scar.'

'I am okay with the scars.'

Satisfied with the counselling, I instructed the staff to shift her into the operation theatre. The surgery started after the induction of anaesthesia. The guru in me awakened. I explained all the steps to Arpit. After finishing one breast, we started on the second one. It was tougher to operate because it was necessary to maintain symmetry in relation to the first one.

'Although we are doing measurements, a lot of subjective judgment is required. So, the surgeons are unlikely to be replaced by robots,' I said to Arpit.

After the surgery, Arpit thanked me profusely. I left happy. Within that month, I operated on a total of six cases at his centre. Suddenly, I realized that Arpit had overtaken me in a short time. I channelized my envy into copying him. Taking a leaf out of his book, my staff was attired in uniforms and a patient counsellor was appointed.

Then, there was a lull *after* the storm. I did not get any call from Arpit's centre for a month. Since his ads were appearing regularly, it seemed that he was doing a good amount of work. Arpit had either become confident or caught hold of some other surgeon. I felt betrayed. However, with time, Arpit and his hospital were a faint memory.

Like a typical surgeon, I worked in spurts. Sometimes, the schedule was back-breaking. However, there were days when there were only a few consultations to be done. On one such lazy day, I reached home early and settled on the recliner. Suddenly, I felt something heavy fall on me. As my eyes opened instinctively, I was delighted to find Saloni sitting on my belly and Nandini supporting her. Both were smiling.

'My darling Papa! How dare you rest without giving your little princess a hug,' Nandini said in a childish voice.

Saloni played with me for a while and then dozed off. Sleep overpowered me, too. A few minutes later, it was interrupted by my mobile phone.

'Hello, is that Dr. Dhruv?' a female voice asked.

'Yes.'

'Doctor, even after messing up my surgery, you did not bother to have a look at me.'

That was a bolt from the blue. I could not recollect any surgery having gone horribly wrong in the last few months.

'If you continue talking like this, I will hang up the phone. There is some sort of misunderstanding. Just tell me the details.'

After my rebuff, the caller mellowed a bit.

'Doctor, I am Romilla Joshi. You operated on me for breast lift two weeks ago at Arpit Hospital. There is a marked difference in size between the right and left side. I have become a nervous wreck.'

'I have not operated on any such case at the Arpit Hospital two weeks ago.'

'Doctor, you met me before going into the operation theatre.'

That was weird. I started feeling dazed.

'I swear I have not operated on you, but I will still try to help you out. Please visit me tomorrow with your discharge summary,' I said, to buy time.

Romilla saw reason and agreed to meet me. I explained the whole situation to Nandini. She looked even more confused than me.

Before meeting the patient the next day, I had to do a fact-finding exercise.

'Should I call that bastard Arpit to get the facts straight?' I asked Nandini.

'There is no use. He will have a cover up story ready,' Nandini said.

I again called on my trusted lieutenant Murari. He was with me in a jiffy.

I told Murari about the strangest complication I had seen in my career. There was no advice about it in any text book or journal.

'Sir, give me some time.'

'The job has to be finished before tomorrow afternoon.'

'That will be possible with the help of shortcuts! Doctor ji, I will get in touch with you as soon as I get some solid information.'

True to his promise, Murari turned up at my office the next morning. His beaming face indicated that he had accomplished the task.

'You are being used. Dr. Arpit is operating independently. However, during difficult surgeries, he uses your name so that the blame is shared in case of a bad result. He makes the patient meet a junior doctor who wears the operation theatre dress which has a label with your name on it. Since the doctor's face is covered with a mask, they are fooled into thinking that they are being operated on by you. The receptionists are also well trained to trap the gullible ones by giving false assurances.'

'How did you find out all this?'

'Through my contacts, I managed to meet Achintya, the operation theatre technician. He spilled the beans to me. Achintya was pained by the malpractice but was keeping mum as he was afraid for his job. Obviously he made me promise not to say it was him. He also revealed that Dr. Arpit overcharges his patients, especially those who need procedure on both sides like eyelids, ears or breast. When the patient enquires about expenses, he quotes an amount. If the patient stays calm, he adds, 'That was for one side!'

'Thanks a lot, Murari. You have done so much for me that I will not be able to repay you in this lifetime.'

'You are welcome, sir. You are our captain and it is our duty to protect you.'

Romilla came in the afternoon. I instantly recognized her as an actor in the hit soap opera *Anokha Parivar*, in which she played the cunning sister-in-law. Acting as my own defense lawyer, I showed her the operation theatre register of my hospital. She was convinced that I had been busy in my own operation theatre when she was being operated at Arpit Hospital.

'Sorry for being rude. I have realized that I have been conned. Doctor, please help me. Since this disaster, I have not been able to shoot. As a result, in the last few episodes of the serial, I have been shown to have gone abroad.'

Examination of her operated area showed a significant asymmetry between the two sites, indicating shoddy work by the surgeon. I worked out a plan for the correction.

'We shall be able to give you a near normal result, but obviously, another surgery will be required.'

'Doctor, please go ahead. It is my fault. If only I had done some research, I wouldn't have fallen into the trap of that crooked doctor.'

I had a lucky escape from a potentially explosive situation. Seething with anger at Arpit, I rang him up and used swear words which I had never uttered previously. Decency could wait!

'Doctor, please calm down. I am really sorry about what has happened. That day, a fault in the laundry caused a shortage of operation theatre linen. So I had to wear the dress with your name on it. The lady mistook me for you. I assure you this mistake will never happen in future because we have arranged for spare operation theatre linen,' Arpit said.

There was no use talking to the scoundrel any further. He was too smart for me. I immediately called Dr. Jayaraj in Dubai and told him about Arpit's hoax.

'Frankly, I did not expect that Arpit would stoop so low. I will reprimand him. Actually, it is his father's fault. He used his money to push him into a profession for which Arpit did not have the aptitude. A greedy surgeon is even more dangerous than a criminal because people go to him willingly and with full faith.'

'Arpit is very innovative. He tricked both me and the patient in one go! The best course of action would be to employ a full time plastic surgeon and let him just oversee the management of the place.'

'Good suggestion. This incident was unfortunate, but it will precipitate a change for the better.'

After talking it out with Dr. Jayaraj, I decided not to take legal action against Arpit. But that incident did push me to the wall as I had already been feeling suffocated due to the advertising blitz launched by newcomers. In trying to outdo each other, they were making outlandish claims.

When I reached home, I became aware of my blessings. Whatever happened at work, I was always welcomed here with warm hugs and genuine smiles.

I told Nandini, 'I am starting to get weighed down by problems.'

She gently stroked my forehead and said, 'Pedestrians often get stuck while crossing a busy road. Some of them get restless because the line of vehicles seems endless.'

'Absolutely.'

'But mostly it is only a wave of traffic and soon you have ample time to cross comfortably. So, just go on with your job and trust me, you will see happier days.'

An Old Wish Resurrected

My fear of fading into oblivion was unfounded. The scope of the job was increasing because more and more people were entering showbiz and required plastic surgery services. The general public was also coming forward for plastic surgery. With the increase of nuclear households, many people had taken control of their lives. Plus, financial freedom was a reality for many women. When their husbands opposed them, they offered to foot the bill for the plastic surgery themselves.

I also started doing certain plastic surgeries which were secretive. Vaginal tightening was often requested by middle-aged ladies. The other procedure, hymen reconstruction, enabled some women to have their cake and eat it too. The love and sex with the boyfriend was followed by *dhokha* with the husband who was made to believe that he was marrying a virgin. Of course, I was also a party to this trickery.

With the sex change operations, I helped men's transition to women and vice versa.

Shagun was in the limelight again. Her fling with newcomer Abhinay was featured in every glossy worth its salt. The fact that none of them had denied it was adding grist to the rumour mills. I reckoned it to be another fictitious romance churned out by Chitra to keep Shagun in the spotlight.

Shagun called me one fine day.

'I want a consultation for a very close friend of mine.'

'Sure. It is your own clinic!'

I instantly recognized Abhinay as he entered my consultation room.

'Hi, this is Abhinay, my fake boyfriend,' Shagun said.

However, the radiance on her face said otherwise.

'I think both of you are more than assumed friends!'

'You are a really keen observer, doc. In fact, she plans more for me than herself,' Abhinay said.

'By the way, Shagun has been very bold in admitting that she knows a plastic surgeon,' I said, with an impish grin.

'We have no secrets between us. She has told me all about her breast enhancement and body shaping. I think you did an awesome job,' Abhinay said.

He had inadvertently revealed that he had explored her fully!

'Thanks. Tell me, what can I do for you?'

'Actually, I require the opposite of what you did on Shagun. Even after pumping a lot of iron, my chest has refused to become flat. Shagun's jeers have also contributed to my decision to go in for plastic surgery. She gifted me her old bra, the one she used to wear before her boob job, with the comment that it would be a perfect fit for my chest!'

After examining him thoroughly, I customized an operative plan for him.

'As a classic case of gynaecomastia, you have excess of fat and gland in the chest. The gland will be removed through an inconspicuous incision. In addition, I will use liposuction to decrease the fat.'

'Doctor, please go ahead. Shagun has blind faith in you and I hope that I will also develop it after the surgery.'

'Since you are going to undergo this surgery under general anaesthesia, may I suggest you an additional procedure which will raise your female fan base like anything.'

'Which kind of male does not want to be popular with the ladies?' Abhinay asked, making Shagun frown.

'You have a flat abdomen but the rectus muscle markings are not so prominent. We can create a six pack look by doing liposuction in a horizontal direction at certain points. Only a little additional operative time will be required.'

'That sounds cool. I can change from a romantic hero to an action hunk just by undressing. Can you do the surgery tomorrow?'

'Sure. Get all the tests and pre-operative check-ups right now. Get admitted in the evening.'

'Relax darling. You are going to be in a homey environment,' Shagun said to Abhinay.

'Doctor, as I was discussing my problem, I figured out that you would look great playing a doctor on television. Our family production house is heavily into television. Just give it a thought.'

'You are making my life difficult with your offer. I will think about it and let you know.'

Abhinay was well motivated for the surgery. But he was mortally afraid of needles. This was not unusual. I had seen many burly men regress into three-year-old kids after seeing an inch long needle!

On the operation day, an intravenous needle was being fixed on Abhinay's hand. Shagun held the other hand. As the needle pierced his skin, he screamed and clutched Shagun's hand tightly. Luckily, the intravenous line was inserted in the first attempt.

'Abhinay, a lady's delicate hands are to be handled with care,' I said.

'Oh! I am so sorry. Shagun, are you okay?' He held Shagun's hand and kissed it.

'I was okay, but it feels even better after your kiss.'

I started Abhinay's surgery with Murari as my assistant. After finishing the right side, I made an incision on the left. At that moment, I noticed blood filling up in the drainage bag on the already operated site. The stitches were immediately opened up. The bleeding blood vessel had to be searched through a small incision which limited access. After five minutes of intense struggle, we found the artery that was causing the trouble. Any more bleeding would have necessitated a blood transfusion.

After the surgery finished, I met everyone with a smile on my face. Talking about the bleeding would have unnecessarily alarmed everyone.

Postoperatively, Abhinay had to take heavy pain-killers.

'Doctor, this is my first and last plastic surgery. I do not think I can go through all this again,' he said.

'Let us see. After a bad hangover, you guys swear not to touch drinks again. But after seeing a shapely whisky bottle, your resolution goes for a toss. Once you start enjoying the new look, the surgical discomfort will be just be a blip in your memory.'

Three weeks after the surgery, Abhinay invited Nandini and me for dinner at the Wave Restaurant in the Golden Sands Hotel. I readily accepted because a friendly get together was the best way to get acquainted.

Abhinay and Shagun were waiting for us at the venue on Saturday evening. They had booked the table on the terrace, which had excellent views. The shimmering lights of the moving ships and boats were a sight to behold.

'Doctor, thanks a ton for the effort you took to make me comfortable. I created a lot of fuss, but you never lost your cool.'

'You conveyed your troubles, but never acted rudely to any of the staff. It's balanced out.'

'I have already started feeling good about my body. By the way, my offer to you for television is still open.'

'I am still undecided about it.'

'I can understand. You have stability in your profession and that's a big plus. But even a strong pedigree does not guarantee me success as a movie actor. You must have noticed that some of the star sons get sidelined at a young age.'

Caressed by the sea breeze, everyone relaxed, and conversation flowed. We had become buddies. I glanced at the northern sky. The stars of The Great Bear constellation were clearly visible.

'Doc, I have noticed that you cannot resist gazing at the sky,' Abhinay said.

He had probably been wondering why I was not paying attention to the two gorgeous ladies on the ground!

'Actually his most beloved deities are present in the night sky! So, he is silently praying to them for getting name, fame and a brand new dame!' Nandini said.

'Let me clarify. Doc is as zealous about astronomy as he is about surgery. His name conveys it all. In fact, he was born a star,' Shagun said.

Eventually we had to say goodbye to each other and promised to remain in touch.

Saloni was going to be three and radiated liveliness. One Sunday, I was playing with her in the living room while Nandini was watching television in the bedroom.

After half an hour of hyperactivity, both of us were exhausted. After Saloni had dozed off, I went to the bedroom to cosy up to Nandini. I gently caressed her hair while she watched a comedy drama on the idiot box. After a while, I was also engrossed as the show was genuinely hilarious.

'Hey, what is wrong with you? You always call television serials junk food for the soul!'

'It is never too late to start fresh in your life. Both of us will have something else to talk about.'

I focused on the sitcom again. The family patriarch, who had the best lines, was stealing the show. Then an idea hit me like a thunderbolt. My brain started firing. Nandini noticed that I was looking at the television, but my mind was not on it.

'What is it, darling? I hope I have not said anything to upset you.'

'Not at all. Actually, I have got a brilliant idea while watching this show. There is a place for Dad in television. He could shine in character roles, especially as the head of a family. Abhinay has made me an offer. I will request him to give Dad a break instead.'

'Are you sure that he will be willing to be an actor at this stage?' Nandini said.

'I am confident that he would make a dash to Mumbai in whatever clothes he is wearing!' I said.

I fixed up a meeting with Abhinay the next morning. The matter was too crucial to be discussed over phone.

I told him the whole story about Dad's stifled ambitions.

'I will do my level best to give him a break. Of course, we are on the lookout for talented actors too. Just tell him to come to Mumbai so that I can have him meet the producers and directors,' Abhinay said.

Buoyed by his positive response, I called Dad straightaway.

'I know you will not believe this! There is an opening for you as a television actor. Come over to Mumbai quickly and leave the rest to me.'

'God is great! I will discuss with your mom and get back to you soon.'

'Dad, you have to take this chance. This may sound rude, but we are not going by Mom's advice.'

Over the past few years, Mom had started dominating Dad. Leaving nothing to chance, I decided to talk to her directly.

'Hi Mom. Dad must have talked about my plan.'

'Do not underestimate me. I was solidly behind you when you chose to make a move to Mumbai. I will not be a hindrance to your dad either. It is important that I stand by him because I know his strengths as well as vulnerabilities.'

'Thanks a lot, Mom.'

They started for Mumbai the very next day.

As I was bringing them home from the airport, Mom said, 'The last time Rajinder was this thrilled was when he received the first love letter from me.'

'People in marooned areas go crazy after they see food packets being air-dropped. My state of mind is more or less the same,' Dad added.

Abhinay was gracious enough to spare a full day to accompany Dad to see the people who mattered in television. Another day was spent at auditions.

'So, how did it go?' I asked Dad.

'Not bad. My previous theatre experience came in handy. There were the usual words of appreciation from everywhere, but no commitment. Perhaps they were afraid to say a blunt no to Abhinay's face,' Dad said, while pouting in disappointment.

'Relax. The final verdict is not out, as yet.'

The following day, we eagerly awaited Abhinay's call. By evening, our faces were despondent. Finally, after dinner, Abhinay called.

'Doc, I had a busy day. Shall get back to you by tomorrow evening,' Abhinay said.

Later, I told Dad, 'It seems that Abhinay is buying time to sugar coat the bitter pill he is going to make us swallow.'

'The fire that you have ignited is not going be extinguished so easily. I will not leave Mumbai without putting up a fight. If there is no response from these people, I will make rounds of other production houses,' Dad said.

He clenched his jaw so tightly that I could hear sounds of his teeth grinding against each other. Just a few hours ago, he had seemed to be mutely resigned to his fate.

Abhinay entered my house with a big grin the next day.

'Congrats Uncle! You are going to be a big shot. Most producers and directors thought very highly of you. Dhanraj, the director of *Sab Chalta Hai*, wants to cast you right away as the jolly grandfather.'

Dad got up from the chair and gave Abhinay an energetic bear hug.

'Oh! You almost fractured my ribs!' Abhinay said.

'It seems that you have never experienced a real hug,' Dad replied.

His rustic humour had resurfaced after a long time.

'Although Uncle has bagged the role on his own merit, Dr. Dhruv deserves the credit, because the whole exercise was his idea,' Abhinay said.

Dad commented, 'This is nepotism in reverse. A son has promoted his father. Who says that only daughters are concerned about their parents?'

'We can never repay you for what you did for us. I am realizing this after becoming a parent,' I said and then bent forwards to touch Dad's feet.

But he stopped me midway and hugged me, rattling my ribs too!

'Dad, actually you don't have to do much acting. Just be yourself and the hilarity will flow!' I said.

'The shooting for the serial will start after two weeks. So, you have to shift to Mumbai by then,' Abhinay told Dad.

We requested Abhinay to join our family celebration but he excused himself.

Dad was so jubilant that he was constantly humming his favourite Mohammed Rafi songs. We decided to celebrate at home so that everyone could let their hair down. As this bash was dedicated to Dad, I arranged for authentic Tandoori food although I had to travel fifteen kilometres for that. Saloni participated by playing pranks.

By the next day, the euphoria had waned a bit. The focus had shifted to the logistics of moving to Mumbai.

'Both of us have decided to rent a separate flat,' Dad said firmly.

'But why? There is enough space in this flat and even more in our hearts.'

I felt bad for being branded as too incompetent to take care of my old parents.

'Son, I am not disputing that at all. We will be much better off in a flat near the studio. Plus, you and Nandini need some privacy at this stage of your married life,' Dad explained.

I could have persuaded my parents to stay with me. However, I reckoned that the crazy Mumbai traffic would be too much for Dad to handle, so, I reluctantly consented.

'But staying away from Dhruv might lead to raised eyebrows among our relatives,' Mom argued.

'Not an issue. Just tell them that my daughter-in-law, Nandini is very quarrelsome. So, it is not possible to stay more than a few days with her!' I said, with a naughty smile.

'Mummy ji, he is pulling our legs,' Nandini said.

Mom kissed Nandini on the forehead and said, 'How dare you make fun of her. She has endeared herself so much to us that we are not even missing Bhavya.'

'You people always take Agrim and Nandini's sides. In an exchange offer, you have given up your son to get a daughter, Nandini and substituted your daughter to get a son, Agrim!'

'It seems that a soap opera is being played out right here in our home,' Dad said in a stern voice and put a full stop to our absurd discussion.

Mom and Dad left in the evening with the intent of coming back in a week. After a long time, I felt at peace. As I moved to embrace Nandini, she turned her back to me.

'So, you have to put up with a bad tempered wife?'

'Yes. But I cannot leave her because I love her like crazy and nobody else would care so much for her.'

Her feigned annoyance evaporated on hearing that.

My parents quickly acclimatized to the oddities of Mumbai.

'As per medical terminology, my life can be called anomalous. At an age when most people live life in the slow lane, I am trying to move to the fast lane,' Dad said.

But even a committed actor like him suffered teething troubles. It took him a while to adapt to multiple retakes in front of bright studio lights. He also had to carry on with fellow actors, some of whom tried to show their stature by throwing tantrums.

The first episode of his show aired two weeks after shooting. All of us were gathered in my house for the curtain raiser. We were soon splitting our sides at the laugh a minute show. I looked at Dad. His masculine instinct seemed to hold back tears of joy. As the episode finished, Dad and Mom were flooded with congratulatory calls. There were a few for his son too!

I went back to my shrine of narcissism the next day. I had already announced Dad's television debut. To my surprise, many employees commented on the inaugural episode. Everything had come full circle. I would be known as the son of Rajinder Khanna again, while for the last few years my dad had been known as the father of Dr. Dhruv Khanna.

My New Look

A national conference on plastic surgery started in Mumbai.
I started bumping into my conference friends. The real life
experiences that we shared were as valuable as going through
books and journals.

In the evening, I looked for liposuction equipment at the
trade exhibition. The repeated movements of the arms during
liposuction caused cramps. It was only a matter of time before
I got shoulder stiffness, back pain and arthritis of the knee, the
other remainders of a surgical career.

I selected a motorized liposuction machine and confirmed
the order.

While checking out surgical instruments at another stall, I
felt a pat on my back. It was Dr. Santosh, the plastic surgeon
whose wife had reprimanded him two years ago for getting
himself injected with fillers without her consent.

'How is the cutting going on?' I asked.

'Cutting is fine, but I am in a fix.'

'You must have noticed that I have developed a paunch.
Some of my clients point it out to me. The brash ones even ask
me why I have not had it corrected.'

'I understand. What they actually mean is that you should practice what you preach. Another reason for you to get liposuction of the abdomen is that you should be able to see your joystick! The conference finishes in two days. After that, I can operate on you, but only after permission from your wife.'

'It seems that you are sitting idle these days!' Santosh said on a lighter note.

'I am only trying to help you,' I replied.

'The truth is that I am scared of undergoing the procedure. I need some time to come to terms with it,' he said.

'Relax. All friends will meet at dinner time. Then, we will surely find a way out.'

'I am afraid that all that you people will do is to laugh at my expense.'

'Laughter is the best medicine and you do social service by doling it out for free!'

'See you.'

After reaching home, I looked at myself in the mirror. My face showed just a slight touch of ageing. But the baggy lower eyelids were crying for attention.

'Patients sometimes do comment on the bags under my eyes. Why not get the correction,' I said to myself.

'I was under the impression that only ladies romanced the mirror!' Nandini said, surprising me.

I had been so lost in my thoughts that I hadn't even noticed her sauntering into the room.

'Actually I was observing the bags under my eyes. I think I need to get them fixed.' I cautiously solicited her opinion.

'It looks like you have been possessed by the idea. Then why wait?'

The festival season was just round the corner. It was supposed to be a lean period for the surgeons. So, there was an opportunity to squeeze in my surgery. I chose Dr. Kale because he had a special interest in plastic surgery of the eyelids. He gave me an early date.

Before the surgery, I needed evaluation for getting fitness for anesthesia. While undergoing the blood tests, I was seized by the fear of testing positive for AIDS and Hepatitis. There had been rare instances of surgeons contracting these diseases due to needle pricks during surgeries they had done on infected patients. Even if all patients were tested pre-operatively, the diseases could be missed if they were in the earliest stage. Luckily, all reports came out normal.

One day prior to the surgery, I was admitted in Dr. Kale's hospital. Sleeping pills were given at night to quiet my anxious mind. In the morning, I put on the television but regretted turning it on. The news channel showed grisly images of the dead and injured amidst mangled coaches of a local train. The headlines screamed, 'Another bomb blast in Mumbai.' My first reaction was to find out whether my surgery was on and I called Dr. Kale.

'We will go ahead with your operation at the scheduled time. I have confirmed that all employees have reached the hospital. It is not so easy to break the spirit of Mumbai.'

Just before I was about to hand over my mobile to Nandini, I received a call from my junior, Dr. Sujay.

'Sir, sorry to disturb you at this time but it is an urgent matter. Murari has been injured in the bomb blast. He is adamant that you operate on him. Otherwise, he is out of danger.'

'I will be there in about an hour. Get the operation theatre ready,' I said in a choked voice.

It was unimaginable that Murari was going to be operated for injuries on the same table where he had assisted thousands of cases.

I told Dr. Kale, 'My technician has been injured in the bomb blast. I will have to operate on him urgently. Sorry for the inconvenience.'

Dr. Kale replied, 'I understand. It is commendable that you are standing by your employee.'

I changed my clothes and drove to my hospital at the speed beating light.

I was used to seeing all sorts of injuries but tears welled up in my eyes as I looked at Murari's wounds. He had shrapnel injuries all over the body. In addition, there was a very large wound on the right upper cheek.

'Doctor sahib, please save me. It was I who insisted on calling for you,' Murari said.

He was disturbed but had his wits about him.

'Relax! You are out of danger. We just need to repair your wounds,' I said.

'I went out of the way to help so many patients. Then why did I get this terrible punishment from God?'

That was a question which only an enlightened master could have answered. However, I had to keep his morale up.

'So many people died or lost their limbs. You got away with simple injuries. Is that not a divine miracle? Think positively. In another week or two, you will be back to your normal life.'

'I am not bothered about getting scars on my face. What is tormenting me is the scene immediately after the blast. It is too horrific to be described in words.'

Since I was fasting, I grabbed a quick bite and then entered the operation theatre. It took us a couple of hours to manage his wounds. Almost all of them were contaminated with shrapnel, pieces of cloth and other foreign material. Most wounds were left open after a thorough cleaning. They were to be sutured after few days of dressings. The facial wound was stitched meticulously.

I underwent my lower eyelid reshaping after two weeks. To make it a low key affair, I did not inform anyone except close family members.

The induction of anaesthesia felt like falling into a deep dark abyss. After the surgery finished, I was kept in the recovery for a few hours. As I was being shifted to the room, to my surprise, a number of familiar faces appeared. All my family members plus Chhatre, Shah, Chitra and Shagun had come to cheer me up.

'How did my surgery become an open secret?'

'We had told Nandini to keep us updated,' Chhatre said.

I was discharged the same evening. Dr. Kale warned me not to look into the mirror again and again, as there would be no visible result till one week because of swelling. After four days, I started going to my hospital as a lot of work had piled up. It also took the attention off my eyelids which I had been evaluating in the mirror repeatedly, contrary to Dr. Kale's advice!

One day, the swelling did subside completely. With the correction of the main imperfection, the good features of my face were no longer hidden. I was curious to know Nandini's verdict, but wanted her to say it spontaneously.

For the weekend, Nandini and I planned lunch at the Jade Restaurant. After that, I was to indulge in a rare shopping spree. The feeling of newness was coaxing me to get a trendy new wardrobe.

The restaurant buffet was elaborate. As we took our seats, Nandini made a sad face.

'Hey, what is the matter? Where are you lost?'

'I have a confession to make,' Nandini said.

She lowered her eyes.

'Look me in the eye and talk.'

'I have cheated on you. I...I have...found a new love in my life.'

I felt the earth move under my feet.

Gathering my strength after a great effort, I managed to ask, 'Who is it?'

'He is the new version of Dhruv!' She smiled suddenly and took me by surprise. 'Hey, you look so cool after the surgery. I feel like being wooed by you all over again.'

'Oh! I almost died of shock.'

'Dhruv, we need a second honeymoon! I will settle for nothing less than a week-long vacation in Spiti Valley in Himachal Pradesh.'

'Done. In a few years, you can have another boyfriend that will be an even newer version of me. Then, you can have another honeymoon.'

As the days passed, I enjoyed the compliments, especially from the opposite sex!

Keeping my promise, I worked out a trip to Spiti Valley in Himachal. The journey was tough, but worth every mile. We reached a place which seemed out of this world. The rare human habitations blended into the stark landscape.

Because of the rarefied air, the night sky revealed so many stars that it was difficult to outline the constellations. The Milky Way dazzled in the centre of the sky dome. We were able to empty our minds of stressful thoughts accumulated over the years.

Just after we had returned to Mumbai, I received a call from Ujjwal. The hottest newcomer had swept a number of heroines off their feet. In just a year, his list of exes was as respectable as that of a veteran.

He said, 'Doctor, I need to see you for an urgent surgery.'

I was tired after the long journey, but did not want to miss out on having Ujjwal as my client.

'Come to my clinic in two hours,' I replied.

There was no choice for me but to rejoin the rat race!

During the consultation, he told me, 'I want to get rid of the skin tags in my armpits with the help of laser.'

'But why are you making such a fuss about a minor problem. Where is the urgency?'

'It is between you and me. I am meeting a special guest soon, in my birthday suit!' he said with a crooked smile.

He was rumoured to be dating the uber sexy Sasha.

It took me just fifteen minutes to finish the job.

The diagnosis was confirmed a few days later when Sasha came to me on Ujjwal's recommendation.

'Doc, please create dimples on my face.'

'You already have a thousand watt smile. What more do you want to achieve? Knock out your fans?'

'Ujjwal loves dimples and so do I.'

'Pleasing two people in one go will make it a very rewarding surgery.'

The next day, we took her up. Under local anaesthesia, a small incision was made inside the cheek, through the mouth. A stitch placed from the undersurface of the skin to the inner tissue of the cheek created the dimple instantly. The procedure was repeated on the other side. There was no visible incision on the outside skin.

Initially the dimples were present even at rest. However, after a month, they appeared only when she smiled and looked natural.

I too smiled a lot those days, although without dimples. After a long time, Nandini and I were doing well professionally and financially. Nandini had started working full time in the same hospital she had joined initially.

God's Chosen Creature

Chitra entered my office with a card and a box of chocolates. It was obvious that she was finally going to tie the knot with Sarjeevan.

'At last, both of you will have your lovemaking certified by society! It is good for me too. You will pester me less often!'

'Are you sure that you will be able to attend my wedding? I am worried that you will faint after seeing me in the bridal dress!'

'Chitra, you are so fond of triangles that you want to invent one in your life.'

'Doc, let us stop this nonsense. Both of us should act mature now. I have been promoted as the editor of *Starsworld*.'

'Another feather in your cap. I am so happy for you. You always had it in you to make it to the top.'

'Wait! There is more. I had recommended you to the editor of *Femininity*. She has verified your credentials and agreed to devote one page to plastic surgery in every issue. It will be basically about you answering queries from the readers. Since *Femininity* is the largest selling women's magazine, you will become a household name,' she said, bringing a smile to my face.

'Thanks a ton for keeping your promise.'

Nandini and I attended Chitra's wedding a few days later. A nasty surprise awaited us. Shagun and Abhinay were standing far apart, with new partners. I recognized the action hero Rajeev with Shagun. Abhinay was with Cherlyn. Both Shagun and Abhinay avoided making eye contact with us, so I also left them alone.

'Look at what both of them are up to,' I said to Nandini.

'Don't get unnecessarily bugged. We can't even control our own lives, what can we say of others,' she said.

But the thoughts about the couple kept on bothering me. After all, they were like my extended family. I could not help calling Shagun.

Shagun said, 'Abhinay got close to co-star Cherlyn during the shooting of *Love Mein Sab Kuchh* in New Zealand. The assistant director of the movie leaked the news to me. When confronted, Abhinay rebuked me for being over-possessive. Feeling cheated, I sought refuge in Rajeev's arms.'

'It seems that you have a waiting list of boyfriends, so that you are never without one, even for a day!

'Doc, do not chide me like that. I am already freaked out.'

'Do you hate Abhinay?'

'To tell you the truth, I detest Cherlyn for causing the upheaval in our lives. I am sure that Abhinay will realize his mistake soon.'

Chitra and I concluded that the bickering would not end without mediation. Then, we contacted Abhinay.

'Actually, the supposed romance between me and Cherlyn was a marketing ploy. But Shagun refused to see reason and made me feel suffocated with her mistrustful behaviour. Then, the outdoor shoot happened and Cherlyn occupied the vacuum created by my tiff with Shagun.'

'It takes two to tango! Cherlyn could not have entered your life without you letting her in,' I said to Abhinay.

Both of them were playing power games but still seemed to be in love. We decided to set up a meeting between Shagun and Abhinay. A lot of persuasion was required. Finally they agreed to get together in a month's time because both of them were out of the city on shoots.

Meanwhile, I worked out all the details with the editorial department of *Femininity* magazine. But even filling up one page was no picnic. I had to write in simple language, plus, dispel the myth that plastic surgeons were magicians who could create fairies out of thin air!

After the first column was published, there were a lot of queries from the public. Within a short while, I had my hands full with plastic surgeries. Dr. Dhruv Khanna had become a super brand.

I basked in my success. But there was a flip side too. My schedule became very hectic as most patients insisted that I operate on them personally. The smart ones would not let the anaesthesiologist administer anaesthesia before they saw my face in the operation theatre.

Although the real action was in the operation theatre and the laser room, the outpatient day was crucial too. It was the point of first contact with patients. Since every problem was unique, one had to constantly cerebrate for the optimum treatment plan.

On a frenzied Monday, I reached my OPD early. To satisfy the patients, I had to give them adequate time to heckle my brain!

'First patient please,' I said to the receptionist.

A lady entered and I greeted her with a welcoming smile. However, my gaze became fixed on her face, specifically her large hazel eyes.

'One in a million,' I mumbled.

'Good morning doctor, I am Lavika,' she said, breaking me out of my trance.

I was embarrassed by my unprofessional conduct, but Lavika seemed to be unruffled. She was probably used to seeing men go gaga over her.

'She should have been named *Naina*,' I said to myself.

'Good morning, please be seated.'

'Guess who has referred me to you?' she asked with a mischievous smile.

I was taken aback. Within a few moments of her first meeting with me, she was acting like an old friend. Her question also baffled me. I had acquired a large number of contacts in Mumbai and it was difficult to pinpoint someone.

'Give me a clue,' I said.

'It is someone who came here long after you but has built up more fans.'

'It must be my dad.'

'Good guessing. No wonder doctors are called the cream of the society.'

'Not anymore. Both doctors and cream have fallen out of favour! Nowadays, society salutes the filthy rich man in the black suit, not the genius in the white coat!'

'I disagree. Apart from the few black sheep, you people are more humane than other professionals.'

'So, Dad is keen to consolidate my practice. How did you bump into him?' I asked.

'I met him on the sets of *Hanste Hasaate*. My sister plays his daughter in the serial. Your dad seems to be extremely proud of you. After introducing himself, he bored me with a long oration on your achievements! So I already know you well. In the end, he strongly recommended that I see you and here I am.'

'What is bothering you?' I asked, coming to the point.

'You must have noticed the freckles on my upper cheeks and nose. Since I am a model, I need to conceal them with a thick layer of make up.'

'We have a convenient solution for you. As easy as saying one-two-three! With a single sitting of Q-switched Nd:YAG laser, most of your freckles will disappear. There is no need for admission or anaesthesia. Of course, sun exposure is to be avoided to prevent recurrence in the future,' I explained and then handed the treatment brochure to her.

'Sounds cool.'

'Make a decision after doing your own research. Look it up on the internet,' I told her as I was confident that I had the optimum technology.

'Okay doctor. I will make up my mind and get back to you.'

Before leaving the room she stared into my eyes so as to finish off whatever little resistance was left in me to succumb to her charm!

After finishing all the cases, I told the receptionist, 'Please bring me Lavika's file.'

Actually, I was curious to know Lavika's marital status. To ask her the question directly would have amounted to indecency. The file confirmed that she was married with her husband's name being mentioned as Vikas.

To my intense delight, she did turn up for the treatment. I focused the laser on her freckles. To keep her relaxed during the procedure, I involved her in conversation.

'So, what type of modelling do you do?'

'Mostly ramp modelling but sometimes I do photo shoots and television ads as well.'

'Any particular fashion label you are associated with?'

'Our home label, Kriti. My husband Vikas is a fashion designer. But I also work for other couture houses.'

'I guess, both of you discovered each other at work.'

'Yes! I walked down the ramp, straight into his home!'

After the laser session, I instructed her about the topical medications and precautions. Usually, I told such patients to revisit me only in case of some problem. But I was desperate not to let her go.

So, I quashed my morality and told her, 'I have written you medications for one week. Please see me after that.'

Although I was quite occupied in the week, a constant tug of war was going on in my mind. I could not believe that I had allowed Lavika to compete with Nandini for my affection.

On the day of her appointment, I told the receptionist, 'Lavika takes a long time for consultation. So, tell the next case to wait for some time.'

Lavika entered my office in a midi. She revealed that there was much more to her than just her eyes! Her perfume was a bit too strong for an office visit.

I was afraid that this could be our last meeting. There was no other imperfection which needed any correction.

'Thanks a lot, Doc. I feel so good.'

'Great. Have you been applying your medication regularly?'

'Yesterday, I missed the night dose of both the creams.'

'How could you forget important instructions? You are inviting complications,' I fumed.

'Oh! I am so sorry. The moonless night tempted me to indulge in an astronomy session. I got so engrossed that I forgot to apply the medicines,' she said.

My joy knew no bounds on hearing this and I felt like hugging her.

'Great! I am also passionate about astronomy. I fact, I was looking forward to meet an astronomy hobbyist in Mumbai.'

I extended my hand to her and she shook it. For the next ten minutes, we talked about our experiences in spotting the heavenly bodies. There was a gentle reminder from the receptionist that patients in the waiting area were getting restless.

'Our spouses may think that we are freaks but actually we are the blessed ones. Do keep in touch,' I said.

'We can now call ourselves "The Star Trekkers". Please take my mobile number.'

The ten digit number seemed like the password to nirvana. After three days, I took the initiative and called her. However, she only had a minute or so for me. It was the same story a few other times. One of us was usually occupied. However, my call to wish her a happy new year was a game changer.

'Can we talk about something other than astronomy?' she said, to my unbridled delight.

The sharp lady had realized that I was hesitant to move forward. That was the start of our real introduction to each other. I was surprised that within days, both of us were discussing everything under the sun.

'One of my friends suggested that laser skin rejuvenation works really well. I would like you to give me a few sessions,' she said.

Clearly, she was working out more visits to my clinic.

As she entered my clinic for the next treatment, I noticed that the reception staff gave her special attention. I wondered if some tongues had already started wagging.

'Six sessions of laser facials at interval of three weeks would make your skin radiant.'

'Why don't you continue with touch-ups after that,' she said suggestively.

'Sure,' I replied.

I ordered tea. By then, the staff had come to know the exact amount of sugar and milk she liked in her cup.

I performed the treatment and called her for follow up after a week.

That day, I headed home on a high. Lavika and I seemed to be settling for a strong friendship that was not physical.

As soon as I entered the living room, Nandini said, 'There is a buzz that you have formed a new tea club with just two members – you and your special client!'

I was so stupefied that I almost fainted.

Composing myself, I said, 'Oh! You are talking about Lavika. She started with the treatment of freckles and now comes for facial rejuvenation. She is an amateur astronomer, too. We talk about sky-watching.'

'Interesting! The way to a man's heart is through the sky.'

'Come on. Don't imagine things. The only passion here is for the telescope!'

'I have solid information. You have a lot of well wishers in your hospital.'

'Nandini, I swear. I have never touched that woman.'

'It is only a matter of time before you touch her and then progress to probing. You are not going to meet her again,' she said adamantly.

At that moment, she looked like *Jhansi ki Raani* ready for battle.

'That is a promise. After her next visit, she will never be seen with me,' I said meekly.

I had no choice, because nothing else would have pacified her.

I was curious to know about the traitor in my hospital. But it was risky to ask Nandini, because that would have reopened the sensitive topic.

The first thing I did on reaching the hospital the following day was to call for Murari, my honorary private eye.

'Murari ji, you must be aware of Madam Lavika who comes here for laser treatments. Someone from our hospital has informed my wife that both of us are having an affair, which is totally baseless. Do whatever it takes but find that person soon. Even if the employee is disgruntled, this act is inexcusable.'

Murari thought for a while and then spoke, 'The culprit is in front of you! It was me who rang up Nandini Madam.'

On hearing this, I had a massive adrenaline surge.

'Murari, how could you do this to me? You often say that you would always remain loyal to me,' I said harshly.

'Please calm down and listen to me. Nothing has changed. I did all this for you and your family.'

'What do you mean? You almost caused a war like situation in our house.'

'Doctor sahib, I have seen marriages of many doctors break down because of extra-marital flings. If things continued this way, you and Lavika Madam would have moved beyond the point of no return. The only person who could stop this was Nandini Madam herself. Give me any punishment you feel like,' he said.

I noticed his eyes were becoming moist. The raging fire in my mind was instantly doused by a huge wave of remorse. I hugged him.

'Thank you...again.'

As the date for Lavika's visit approached, I was going through a lot of turmoil.

She came in, wearing a designer outfit, which was shorter than the one she had worn the last time!

'Hey, I have never seen you look so gloomy,' she said.

'A hospital employee has told my wife about our friendship. She has taken it in a wrong way and firmly warned me not to see you again.'

'Our relationship has not been misunderstood! I have been waiting for you to make a move. At every visit, I wished that you would ask me out for lunch.'

'So, what do we do now?' I asked.

She was left with the unpleasant task of pronouncing the death sentence on our relationship.

'Perhaps we were destined to travel only a short distance together. So, let us cherish it and move ahead.'

Trying to justify the episode for both of us, I said, 'A constant battle rages on between morality and attraction. But when a heavenly creature like you appears, ethics go for a six!'

'I wish you a lot of success and happiness in life,' she said.

It was the signal that she was ready to move out of my life forever.

'Same here. I want you to reach for the stars,' I said.

We shook hands and she left with tears in her eyes. She had probably been expecting a parting kiss, but I restrained myself.

When I reached home, I told Nandini, 'Lavika came for the last sitting today. She agreed not to meet me again after I put my foot down!'

'Thanks. I appreciate that.'

The storm had passed without causing major damage. But it was a game changer.

To my surprise, Nandini started sprucing herself up, as if she was partly responsible for my philandering! She got herself a chic hairstyle and started applying makeup regularly. Nights became ethereal, and her sensual negligees only added fuel to the fire.

I decided to channelize my energy in newer pursuits so there wasn't any inclination to go astray. A new technology, endoscopic plastic surgery, beckoned. With the keyhole approach, one could avoid the open incision for many surgeries, especially the brow lift.

One day, while I was engrossed in a book on endoscopic plastic surgery, my mobile beeped. It seemed to be an annoying commercial message. However, I needed a break and checked it. It was from an unknown number, but the contents gave me goosebumps.

It read – 'Doctor, thanks for making me beautiful with your treatments. I can't help thinking about you all the time. 8890956798.'

There was no clue about the identity of the lady who had sent the message, but the immediate reaction was glee.

'I have a way with women!' I said to myself.

However, I could not remember being close to any lady in the recent past apart from Lavika. It seemed to be a brand-new crush from another patient.

'No way. Not again!' I said to myself.

I decided not to reply to the message. In fact, I immediately deleted it lest Nandini read it.

I felt proud of myself for achieving the highest level in mental strength; the ability to resist the temptation of lust. However, I was worried about the sender's reaction to my cold shoulder. What if another message came? But I took solace in the fact that there was no chance of Nandini getting to know it.

At tea time, I and Nandini were chatting casually.

'So, what was special during the day?' Nandini said.

'Nothing. Just the usual work.'

'Even getting hot propositions on your mobile does not excite you!'

'Nandini, this is too much. You seem to have hired a full-fledged spying agency for me.'

'You have invited it on yourself. I cannot afford to take any chances after the Lavika episode.'

'This time I am absolutely innocent. I swear that I do not know the sender. By the way, how did you break into my mobile?'

'No special technology, just some smart thinking! The message was sent from my friend Ishta's mobile. Any call or message from you was to be received and recorded. Anyway, I give you an overall pass in this exam.'

'Oh, come on. I was so thrilled to know that a young girl is infatuated with me! You have spoilt my day by revealing everything,' I laughed.

Finally, I had the long overdue meeting with Shagun and Abhinay, in my office.

'For how long will you play this childish hide and seek game with each other?' I asked angrily.

'Not anymore. We made up just yesterday after realizing that we cannot be apart, even if we want to.'

'Let us see. I will not be able to broker your truce every time.'

'The moral of the story is that it is a must to have an oldie like you as a friend!' Abhinay said.

'Do not add insult to the injury. I am feeling low since morning because one of my patients called me Uncle!'

'Cheer up. We have actually come to thank you. You are our common ground because we talk a lot about cosmetic surgery,' Shagun said.

'So, which character are you portraying next? I really loved your comic act in the last movie, *Gol Gappe*,' I said to Shagun.

'I am playing a seductress in the crime thriller *Toofan Bin Bijli*. There will be lots of scenes in dim lighting. Can you do something to make my face match my character?'

'Full lips and high cheekbones would make for a sexy and mysterious look. I can give filler injections in these two areas. The effect will stay for about six months. By that time, shooting for this movie will finish. Then, you can plan your look for the next role. If you are playing a college girl, I could make your face look more rounded.'

'This is so exciting. I can play around with the contours and features of my face.'

'Nobody is bothered about my look,' Abhinay interrupted.

'You do not have a sensuous pout, cleavage or even sexy legs! So let the spotlight be on me,' Shagun replied.

'What an unfair world for guys. Amongst most birds and animals, the male is showier!' Abhinay said.

New Horizons

I was riding high on fame and recognition. Relatives and friends were coming all the way from Delhi for treatments. It was tricky to operate on blood relations as even minor complications could activate whispering campaigns. But, Dad liked hosting his family. He enjoyed himself the most when they pleaded with him to get an early appointment with me.

'I tell everyone that nowadays it is more important to have a plastic surgeon in the family than an IAS officer!' Dad said to me, when I went to see him on a weekend.

An aunt from Delhi visited me. She had come to Mumbai to meet her sister. I had been warned by my mom to be careful of her because she was very demanding. Satya aunty showed a problem which was more common in thin skinned Caucasian women. She had fine criss-cross wrinkling all over the face.

'Beta, do something about these wrinkles. I have avoided all types of invasive procedures till now. My cousin told me that you could make them less obvious.'

I explored all the possibilities like Botulinum toxin injections, fillers and facelifts. However, her problem seemed to be too advanced for a good result. I started looking for an escape.

I told her, 'These wrinkles are normal for your age. Take them in your stride. Age gracefully.'

'If you say these words to all your patients, you will hardly have any work to do! Do not assume me to be a freeloader. In fact, I will not demand any concessions.'

She made me feel as embarrassed as a thief who had just been caught red handed.

'To tell you the truth, I am not sure of the results. So, I do not want to risk souring our relationship,' I said.

'Go ahead. Do not be afraid. Whatever happens, my face will definitely look better than what it is. Even if I am not happy, the most I will do is pull your ears!'

I performed a mix of therapies on Satya aunty. So much work was bound to show some results.

'How do you feel about yourself now?' I asked her anxiously even though I was pleased with her post treatment appearance.

'You have taken ten years off my face. And I will bring you at least ten more cases. The moral of the story is that a plastic surgeon should never tell anybody to age gracefully. Rather, your motto should be to make people age youthfully!'

I touched her feet and then folded my hands, 'You are peerless! It has been a long time since a patient has got the better of me.'

After seeing aunty's results, my parents also felt bolder. They declared that to look younger was their fundamental right too. But, surgeons are not supposed to cut up their parents because excessive emotional attachment could lead to problems during the surgery. So I let Dr. Kulkarni do their face lifts.

The internet savvy patients, who were increasing in number day by day, needed to be handled with care. The web did help to educate and inform. But, some patients had a know-it-all attitude. They did not realize that a lot of internet knowledge was either superficial or influenced by commercial interests. Those who tried to teach me were shown the door and told to get operated by Dr. Google!

The main casualty of my ever busy schedule was family time. I decided to take Nandini into confidence.

'Honey, my work life balance is going haywire and I am not able to do anything about it.'

'But, you read so many self help books and often quote from them that one's career should not be the only driving force.'

'Agreed. But the Ferrari comes first and only then do people think of renouncing everything to become monks. I have not yet reached the first stage!'

However, there was no way I could convince Saloni. She made faces and then boxed me if I turned home late. And often, she had already dozed off by the time I reached.

Just when life seemed to be settling into a pattern, I got a call from the megastar Rajan's secretary.

'Doctor sahib, Rajan ji wants an appointment with you.'

I was wary of Rajan as previously, he had left me in the lurch by opting to have his surgery done abroad. However, a small fry like me could not ignore the behemoth.

I met him at his home.

'Welcome great plastic surgeon of Mumbai, or should I say India!' he said loudly as I entered his bungalow.

'Thanks,' I answered blandly.

My annoyance was obvious in my cold response.

'The public might worship us, but we can never match your heroics. We can get away with flops, but you have to perform perfectly every time,' he said.

I replied, 'Ordinary people do so many amazing jobs but remain invisible. However, Mr. Rajan makes news even if he catches a common cold!'

I was beginning to open up around him.

'But Rajan also comes into the limelight if he is spotted leaving an actress' flat. He is pronounced guilty of bed hopping even if it is a social call,' he laughed.

'So that means it is not always an innocuous visit!'

'It is said that one should never hide anything from the treating doctor. So I admit that like every male, I do want to retain my appeal to the opposite sex. My face area needs attention.'

'Yes, you are a candidate for an endoscopic brow lift surgery.'

'You must be suspecting that like last time, I have called you for an opinion only. Previously, I opted to be operated abroad because of privacy issues. The result was satisfactory. But, I was a nonentity for the surgeon and the staff. So, I made up my mind to be operated here.'

'It would be my pleasure. But, I cannot assure you about privacy. A rogue hospital employee could tip off the press.'

'Why don't you do it in Dubai? It is just a couple of hours away by flight.'

'That is a brilliant idea. Luckily, Dr. Jayaraj, my guru, has a plastic surgery hospital there. I will get back to you soon.'

After reaching home, I contacted Dr. Jayaraj. He was only too pleased to help me out and worked out all the details to operate in Dubai.

After two weeks, Rajan was at Dr. Jayaraj's hospital. There was minimal use of the knife during the surgery. An endoscope introduced through a keyhole incision did the job.

'Dhruv, why don't you make it once a week to operate here? Live life like a Sheikh!' Dr. Jayaraj said.

'That would be great. I will work it out.'

'Take your time.'

As I was flying back, I looked down on the blue waters of the Arabian Sea. Could a jet setting lifestyle be the next step in my life? On weekends, I could start off with breakfast in Mumbai before flying to Dubai and operating there. The grand finale would be a night cruise on the Seine in Paris where Nandini and I would enjoy Cabernet Sauvignon.

Back home, I told Nandini about the new development.

'You have become "Mr Hurry!" I have no choice but to keep pace with you.'

Another superstar called on me the next day. Malavika was rumoured to command a fee as high as some of the top heroes. I met her in my back office after making her come via the secret entrance. It was her first consultation with me although I had met her a few times at parties.

'I admire you for starting the trend of heroine-centric movies.'

'The cold hard truth is that heroines have to retire early, while male actors, in their forties and fifties keep on romancing teenagers.'

'Now, we have the ways and means to extend the expiry date.'

'Do something about the wrinkles on my face. They require more and more grease paint. Otherwise, find me a handsome, filthy rich NRI groom so that I can say goodbye to the film industry!'

'Don't panic. You have come to the right place. A thread lift under local anesthesia will tighten your face and delay facelift for a few years. In addition, you will need fillers and laser skin rejuvenation. I would also like to give Botulinum toxin injections selectively, so that your ability to emote is preserved. After all, you do need to frown while acting.'

'Start with the treatments right away.'

Since she did not require any admission, we finished all the procedures in a single day and sent her home. By her first follow up visit, her charm was greatly enhanced.

'Doctor, I am really pleased because I have gained a lot in a short time. Can I disclose your name if I talk to the media about my plastic surgery?'

'Please do. In fact, that would be a big favour to me,' I replied.

A month later, her minor procedures created a major stir. In an interview in *Star Mantra* magazine, she confessed to having undergone aesthetic procedures. Never before had a star openly admitted to taking the help of a plastic surgeon. She had even mentioned my name.

When she came for her last follow up, I said to her, 'Malavika ji, you have maintained your trend-setting streak. After your disclosure, plastic surgeons will come out of the shadows.'

'I was the first to appear in a two-piece bikini on screen. That paved the way for heroines to celebrate their bodies. People speculate about what is going on behind closed doors. I just brought it out in the open.'

'Very true,' I commented.

'I have a question for you. Is there any end to aesthetic procedures? I mean where to stop? There is a danger that one could get pre-occupied with battling wrinkles,' she said.

'Just follow your heart. As long as you are enthusiastic about it, indulge in it. Time ultimately wins. It gets the better of every anti-ageing procedure. A stage will come in your life when looks will not matter. That is the time to show off the grey hair of wisdom and wrinkles of experience.'

Within a few days of the publication of Malavika's interview, the waiting list for being operated on by me increased to more than one month. I had my own permit raj and often operated on the influential ones out of turn. The heavy workload caused so much fatigue that sometimes I needed pain killers.

However, one morning, the back pain was present even after a full night's rest. It seemed to have been caused by overwork. Since it was not possible to rest, I increased the dose of the analgesic.

In the evening, the pain started radiating from my back to my buttocks and then to my legs. It was obvious that either a slipped disc or a tumour was pressing on my spinal nerves. I told my orthpaedician friend, Dr. Suryajit, about the symptoms.

'Why don't you come to my hospital tomorrow morning and we will have a look,' he said.

Despite his reassurance, I felt a sense of impending doom.

As I was entering Suryajit's office, his gaze was fixed on my walk.

'Your gait makes me think it is a slipped disc. A plain X-ray and MRI need to be done to confirm the diagnosis.'

'I will see you in the evening after getting the results,' I said.

'You have invited this problem on yourself by ignoring the early warning signs. Doing lengthy surgeries has put additional stress on your back.'

'I assumed that my back was just malingering! Coincidentally, this was when my career had started peaking,' I said.

I was hoping against hope that the MRI might be normal. However, the report left me speechless. There was prolapse of not one, but two discs in the lower backbone.

Suryajit looked at the MRI films.

He said grimly, 'Have complete bed rest for a minimum of three weeks. This may possibly extend to six weeks. Most likely that will settle your problem, but surgery cannot be ruled out.'

I said, 'My career could be put back by at least a couple of years.'

'I understand your concern, but take it positively. You will have so much free time that some radical idea might occur to you.'

At home, Nandini suggested that we get more opinions. I readily agreed. Dreading that I would have to spend the next few weeks in the company of pillows, I fervently tried to find an escape. We went to two orthopaedic surgeons and a neurosurgeon as well. The opinions varied but all of them agreed that initially, I should have complete bed rest for three weeks.

With a heavy heart, I cancelled all the pending appointments for surgeries. Dr. Kulkarni agreed to help me out by following up my old cases.

The first day was not too bad. Nandini had taken leave to be with me and I also informed my friends of the circumstances. A constant stream of visitors kept me occupied.

Three days later, Chitra and her husband visited.

'Life is so uncertain. I feel worthless,' I said gloomily.

'A surgeon never gives up even when the odds are against him. So, by our next visit, we want you to be the old jovial Dr. Dhruv. Do activate your Facebook account and connect with your old pals. That will make you feel better,' Chitra said persuasively.

On her advice, I started a Facebook account. Within a few days, I had a big list of lost and found pals.

My first post was: 'Having a long vacation courtesy my slipped discs.'

My Facebook page was flooded with messages wishing me an early recovery. The best one was from my schoolmate Sanjay. While establishing a new business, he had to work long hours.

Sanjay wrote, 'Oh God, give me a break too, even if it is through a slipped disc!'

Three weeks passed. There was only partial relief from the pain and stiffness. After repeat investigations, my remand was extended for another three weeks. I came home and told my parents about the situation.

'The strain of doing surgery is playing havoc with your back. It is high time you took to acting. In India, few get a chance to change their profession. I am well established in television. So, you will have it easy right from the beginning,' Dad said.

'Thanks Dad. Give me some time to think it over.'

This time it did make sense to switch careers. If I continued to perform surgical operations, there could be worsening of my back problems. From my US trip, I remembered Dr. Michael Walters, the aeronautical engineer who had switched his career at a late age. I felt him whisper to me, 'Come on Dhruv. Follow your heart, not conventions.'

To clear up my confusion, I called Dr. Vidur. Luckily, he was due to visit Mumbai in a few days to attend a conference.

He dropped in at my place prior to the conference.

'It is the same old story. Surgeons spend their prime in training and a few years more to make their mark. By the time they reach their peak, the wear and tear starts showing on their body,' the chief said.

'That is why I am planning to retire from surgery and become an actor.'

I told him about my dad's proposal.

'This is just escapism. Look at me. I also suffered a slipped disc fifteen years ago and had to take traction. But I recovered fully and have managed to prevent a recurrence by doing back exercises. Then, there is the example of Dr. Mohan who suffered a heart attack twelve years ago but is still working with the zeal of a youngster. My students are fighters, not wimps. I am sure that you will be back in the operation theatre within a few days doing what you like best,' Dr. Vidur said passionately.

'Sir, I really appreciate you for helping me out of this mess.'

'I take a lot of pride in my students. They are my wealth. So I consider myself an individual with a high net worth.'

The chief's motivation made me feel positive. The same day, Shagun and Abhinay also visited me. Shagun was adamant on my picking up the scalpel again.

She said, 'Who will take care of our looks? We will require even more of your help as we age.'

I went to see my orthopaedician friend after the stipulated rest period. Repeat investigations did show that the problem had subsided to a great extent.

'You escaped my operation table by a whisker! Start your work, but go slowly. By all means, take some time for back exercises.'

At home, Nandini told me, 'I will have to act as your nurse, too. From now on, I will ensure that you do not miss physiotherapy. '

The next day, I had a word with Dr. Vidur, who was still in Mumbai.

'Back is better. My orthopaedician has given me a clean chit. So, I plan to join my duty tomorrow. Why don't you pay me a visit? There have been so many changes in the hospital since you last came.'

'I was thinking the same thing.'

The hospital staff gave me a rousing welcome and I did the same for Dr. Vidur.

'I have no doubts now,' I declared.

'You have a long surgical career left. Just think of the future possibilities. One day, you might perform DNA surgeries to change people's looks. Various tissues and body parts will be custom made for you in a lab. Gene therapy and stem cells will enable you to do things which are unthinkable today. In short, you will play God. Well, almost,' the chief said.

A week later, my dad announced that he finally managed to get the lead role in a movie about the lives of a retired couple. That day, I felt an ethereal calm like never before.

As for me, I will continue to annoy God by altering his creations, until he pronounces, 'Enough is enough. Summon this chap to me!'

Recommended Reading

Life is What You Make It

Preeti Shenoy

"A simple narration with umpteen smart phrases makes the book a one session reading."
– The Times of India.

"This book promises to be a show stealer."
– Deccan Chronicle

What would you do if destiny twisted the road you took?

What if it threw you to a place you did not want to go?

Would you fight, would you run or would you accept?

Set across two cities in India in the early eighties, this book is a gripping account of Ankita Sharma's life, who has the world at her feet. She is young, good-looking, smart and has tons of friends and boys swooning over her. But six months of being in a premier MBA college, she is a patient in a mental health hospital.

How did Ankita get here? What were the events that led to this? Will she ever get back her life?

It is a deeply moving and inspiring account of growing up, the power of faith and how determination and an indomitable spirit can overcome even what destiny throws at you.

Preeti Shenoy is an author and an artist based in Bangalore, India. She also specializes in pencil portraits and holds an internationally recognized qualification from UK in portraiture.

ISBN: 978-93-80349-30-5, Price: ₹ 120, Pages: 224, Binding: Paperback

Googled by God

Pulkit Ahuja

This is a fast moving financial thriller that takes the reader on a journey to the dark realms of entrepreneurship and technology. Revolving around the ever changing worlds of stock markets, investments and money, the reader soon finds himself in the middle of a dangerous game of emotions and karma.

Pulkit Ahuja is a serial entrepreneur with experience in founding and running disruptive technology start-ups in education, ad-tech and transportation domains. He is an MBA Gold Medallist in Finance, formerly associated with Standard and Poor's Capital IQ.

ISBN: 978-93-82665-44-1, Price: ₹ 195, Pages: 178, Binding: Paperback

Ready..Steady..Exit

P.C. Balasubramanian

Gautam completed CA after several attempts and to his luck, landed up with Anand, a close friend and brilliant CA, to launch an Accounting Services company named FAB. When Vimal comes in with a delectable package, an impressive consulting profile and his smart and very beautiful sister Ruchi, FAB grows… but relationships deplete.

This book is a humorous, dramatic, romantic, enlightening and entertaining read.

P.C. Balasubramanian (PC to some and Bala to others) is a Chartered Accountant by qualification and an author by accident. He is one of the promoters and directors of Matrix Business Services India P Ltd, and has to his credit two bestsellers.

ISBN: 978-93-82665-40-3, Price: ₹ 120, Pages: 184, Binding: Paperback

It Doesn't Hurt to be Nice

Amisha Sethi

This is Kiara's story and the wisdom she achieves through the various dramatic and hilarious experiences, as much as it is yours. *You* are the 'hero' of the book, who can beat the most stubborn of villains…our fear, unkindness, selfish interests, negative thoughts and jealousy. *You* are the 'heroine' who is sharp and witty in talking, selfless and caring in love, and charming and beautiful inside out, like none other (perhaps a 2.0 version of you).

Amisha Sethi is an executive scholar from Kellogg School of Management, Northwestern University, Chicago, and holds an MBA degree in Marketing from Amity Business School. She was awarded the "Young women rising star" at World Women Leadership Congress 2014.

ISBN: 978-93-82665-48-9, Price: ₹ 175, Pages: 144, Binding: Paperback

The Great War of Hind

Vaibhav Anand

Around 12000 B.C., Hindustan as we know it today (or Hind), comprised five kingdoms of man, sandwiched between Parbat – the kingdom of the Gods in the north, and Lunka – the kingdom of the demons in the south. The 'Legend of Ramm' unravels the story of the military general called Ramm in the kingdom of Ayodh and how his actions came to define our world as we know it today.

Vaibhav is a marketing professional working with an MNC by day, blogger/ writer/ poet by night. Author of the bestselling If God Went to B-School, Vaibhav is also one of the top contributors to Faking News, the satire portal.

ISBN: 978-93-82665-46-5, Price: ₹ 175, Pages: 184, Binding: Paperback